Goodnight, San Francisco

By

H. P. Oliver

MYSTERIES IN HISTORY

HPO Productions
8698 Elk Grove Boulevard
Suite 1-271
Elk Grove, California 95624

Cover art and design by Steve Eitzen

Back cover author photo:
1937 Chrysler Imperial Business Coupe owned by Camela and Dave Labhard and displayed at the California Automobile museum in Sacramento, CA. Photograph by Tim McCoy.

Printed in the United States of America

ISBN-10: 0988833158
ISBN-13: 978-0-9888331-5-9

DEDICATION

For Jean and Pete

ACKNOWLEDGMENTS

The author wishes to thank the Bay Area Radio Hall of Fame and the San Francisco Radio Museum for their invaluable assistance in researching this book and for their dedication to preserving the radio heritage of San Francisco, the birthplace of radio broadcasting. Thank also to Suzanne Cox for her considerable patience and skill at keeping the author's wayward commas in check.

PLEASE NOTE

This book occasionally refers to individuals and groups with terms that are considered inappropriate in today's society. These terms, however, were in common usage during the historical period in which this story is set and are included here solely for the purpose of accurately depicting the attitudes and customs of the era.

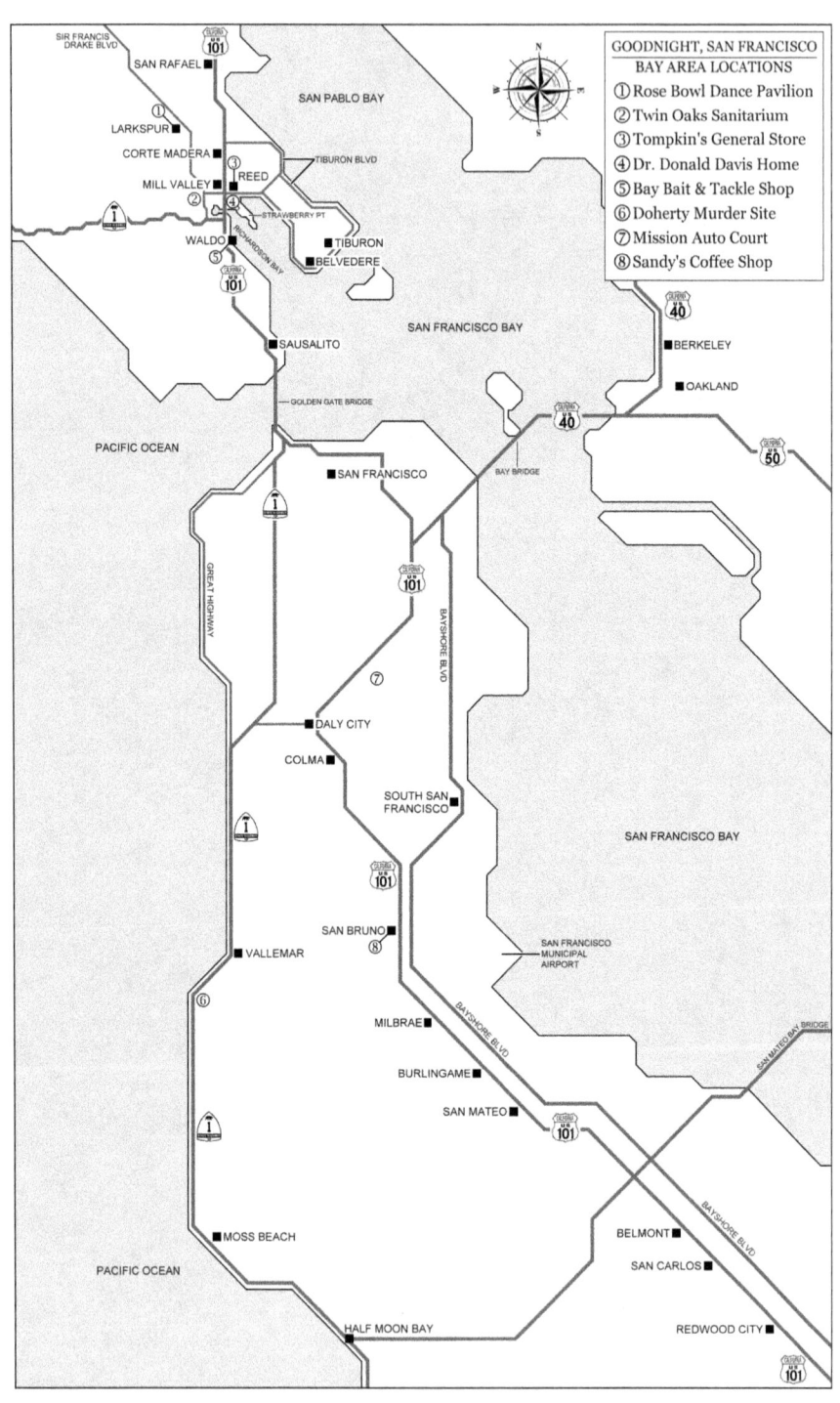

GOODNIGHT, SAN FRANCISCO
BAY AREA LOCATIONS
① Rose Bowl Dance Pavilion
② Twin Oaks Sanitarium
③ Tompkin's General Store
④ Dr. Donald Davis Home
⑤ Bay Bait & Tackle Shop
⑥ Doherty Murder Site
⑦ Mission Auto Court
⑧ Sandy's Coffee Shop

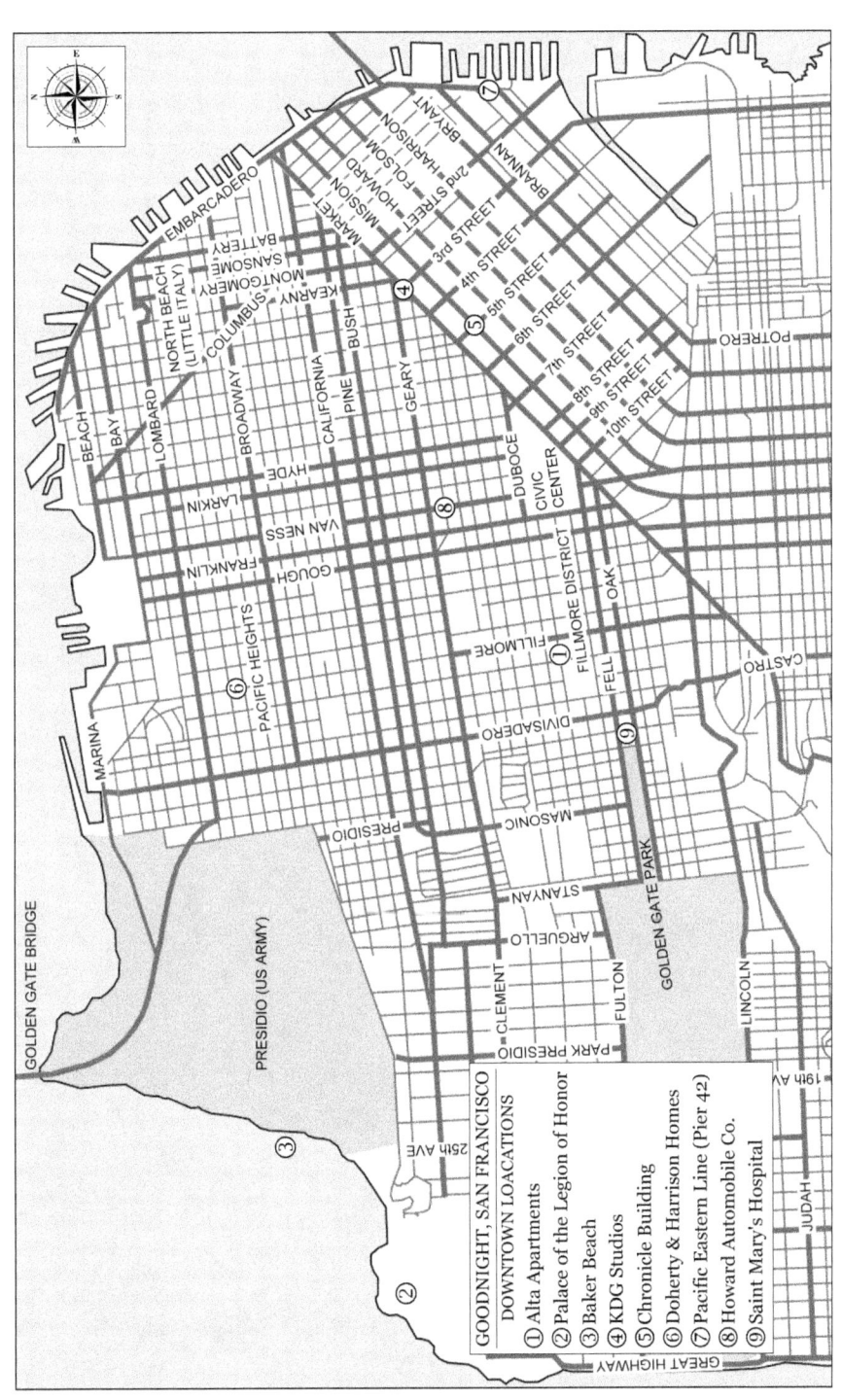

Goodnight, San Francisco

One

3:00 a.m.—Sunday—June 6, 1937

In the wee small hours, California Highway One north of Half Moon Bay is about as desolate as it gets. The narrow, twisting road was etched from sheer cliff faces that towered above me on the right and dropped away a hundred feet to the Pacific Ocean on my left.

A soggy wool blanket of San Francisco's famous fog hung a few feet above the roadway, obscuring the stars and dribbling tiny spots of mist on my windshield. My headlights bored through the gap between road and fog, drilling an endless tunnel through the darkness.

So far as I could tell, there were only two other cars on the entire planet that night—actually, one car and a produce truck. They'd flashed by, one after the other, heading south just past Moss Beach. Their headlights glared in my eyes and made the road seem even narrower, but half an hour later, I was wishing for more signs of life just to help keep my drooping eyelids from slamming shut altogether. It was the wrong thing to wish for.

She appeared suddenly out of the fog on the opposite side of the road. Only, she wasn't in a car. This gal was smack dab in the middle of the southbound lane and running for all she was worth. She wore a white dress and no coat, and that was about all I had time to take in before she was gone and I was alone in the endless tunnel again.

I shook my head in disbelief and stared into the rear view mirror. A vague white blur in the glass contradicted my absolute certainty that I was seeing things, but it took a few more seconds for my drowsy brain to hatch the idea that a woman running down this desolate stretch of road at three in the morning might need some help.

We'd passed each other near the bottom of a long uphill grade, and I was almost to the top before I found a place to turn around. It was one of those wide spots on the right shoulder where slow trucks and timid drivers are supposed to pull over and let the accumulated traffic behind them go by.

I pulled off and cranked the steering wheel around, but as I let out the clutch, a pair of brilliant lights topped the hill a hundred feet further up the road. I slammed the brake pedal to the floor and a large, dark Lincoln Zephyr flashed through my headlights. A big man wearing a hat was hunched over the wheel as if he were concentrating on the road ahead. I hoped to hell he was concentrating, because at that speed, the woman at the bottom of the hill would appear in his headlights without any warning, giving him precious little time to avoid hitting her.

Loose gravel spattered against the underside of my Ford coupe' as I stomped on the throttle and sped off in pursuit of the Lincoln. For a moment I had the absurd notion that I might be able to catch the guy and slow him down, but his taillights were fading into the darkness much too quickly. My eyes were fixed on those two vague pinpoints of pink light as I accelerated down the hill. I willed them to grow larger. Instead, they suddenly veered to the left. He'd seen the woman and swerved to miss her!

In the same instant something white flashed through the air to the left of the Lincoln's taillights. I screamed at my windshield, "You son of a bitch!" Of course, the driver of the Lincoln couldn't hear me. He couldn't even see me in his rear view mirror anymore. He was already around the bend beyond the bottom of the grade.

A sick feeling heated up my gut as I slowed to look for her body. There was no question about it. The guy in the Lincoln hadn't swerved to avoid the woman; he'd gone out of his way to hit her.

I turned across the highway and pulled in close to the cliff. My headlights showed her there, sprawled against the rocks. She'd picked a lousy dress to die in. Dark stains were already showing through the thin white material in several places and one sleeve was torn to the shoulder, exposing bare pale skin to the early morning chill.

She had no pulse that I could find, and when I put my ear to her chest, I heard nothing but hollow emptiness. I stepped back and listened to breakers crashing against the rocks below the highway instead.

The dead woman stared up at me through dull hazel eyes, framed by short brown hair that was dark and matted on one side. A rivulet of dark red blood wound down her cheek and dripped steadily from her chin onto the white dress.

Even in life I wouldn't have called her a raving beauty, but she wasn't unattractive, either. Mostly, she was just a woman in her late twenties or early thirties with an average figure and regular features. Her clothes and jewelry were another matter, though. The torn shoulder of her dress revealed an I. Magnin label and the teardrop pendant hanging from a gold chain around her neck was surrounded by clear stones that sparkled brightly in my headlights. I'm no expert, but I know expensive when I see it, and this gal was definitely Nob Hill.

My car robe covered everything but her ankles and feet. I could have used my jacket to cover the rest of her, but the damp air had a knife-edge to it that bothered me a lot more than it did her, so I left the jacket on and thought about getting some help. Calling an ambulance wasn't going to do her any good, but getting someone after that Lincoln seemed like a smart idea. The problem was, I couldn't call anybody without a telephone, and I couldn't just leave her lying there while I went off to look for one.

I was pondering this dilemma when a low rumble grew out of the surf noises. It was coming from the south and sounded like a big engine of some kind. I wondered for a moment if the Lincoln was coming back. After a few seconds, though, I quit worrying about the Lincoln. What was coming was a truck, and with my car sticking out into his lane less than fifty feet from the blind curve at the bottom of the hill, the driver was in for one hell of a shock when he rounded the bend.

There wasn't time to move my car. Sprinting downhill, I got to the curve just before he did and started wig-wagging my arms over my head. The truck's headlights hit me full in the face, and as I dodged to the side of the road, a lot of screeching and grinding filled the air while the driver fought to keep his rig from sailing off into the drink.

When he got the truck stopped, the driver came charging down from his cab like John L. Lewis going after a strikebreaker. He was big, hairy and mad.

"What the hell's the matter with you, buddy? Ya almost got us both killed!"

Holding my hands up in what I hoped look like an apologetic gesture, I said, "Sorry. I was trying to get you to slow down before you ran into my car over there."

He glanced at my Ford. "Why in blazes did ya stop in a stupid place like that to begin with?"

"There was an accident here a few minutes ago. A woman got hit by a car and I was trying to help."

That put the whole picture in an entirely different light. Suddenly the driver was full of concern. "A woman? Is she okay? Where's her car?"

"She wasn't in a car, and she's dead."

"What do ya mean, 'she wasn't in a car'?"

"Just what I said. She's over here."

I pulled a corner of the car robe back and he swore. "Shit! What the hell happened?"

"She was running down the southbound lane over there when I passed her going north, but before I could get turned around, somebody came roaring down the hill and hit her."

He turned away from the broken woman under my car robe and shook his head. "Sweet Jesus! What do ya suppose she was doin' out here all by herself?"

"Damned if I know, but I've got to report this to the cops. Is there a telephone up the road somewhere?"

"Yeah, there's a public phone outside the roadhouse at Vallemar Station."

"I don't want to just go off and leave her. How 'bout you call the cops and I'll wait for 'em here?"

"Sure. I'm on my way." The driver turned and jogged off toward his truck, but halfway there, he stopped and turned around. Anger was creeping back into his voice again as he asked, "Say, you didn't hit that gal, did ya?"

"No. It was somebody in a big Lincoln. He was headed south. Maybe you passed him."

"Yeah, I saw him, alright. A big black sedan . . . he went by me a ways back down the road, goin' hell-bent for leather."

"Well, get to that phone as fast as you can so we can send the cops after him."

I listened to his engine straining up the hill, and when his only working taillight disappeared over the crest, I jotted the truck's license plate number in my notebook. It occurred to me that the cops might get the same idea about who hit the woman. At least the truck driver could vouch for the fact that there really was a speeding Lincoln out here tonight.

4

Leaning against a fender that was damp from the fog, I listened for traffic and wondered about the woman and why she'd been killed. When I didn't come up with any good answers, my mind drifted back to another time . . . a time when I carried a shiny gold badge and dead bodies were part of my job. Sadly or gratefully, depending on how you looked at it, most of the images that remained in my mind from that time are little more than hazy pencil sketches worn thin by an eighty-proof eraser.

I've learned to avoid looking at those pictures, but sometimes my brain doesn't cooperate. This was one of those times, and I was glad when a couple of wailing sirens finally drove my dark memories back into their hiding place.

Two patrol cars converged on me from opposite directions. They got there within seconds of each other, and the sergeant, who'd come from the north, took command of the situation. He was short and stocky with a fringe of gray hair showing around his khaki uniform cap. The other fellow was tall, sharp-featured, and couldn't have been more than twenty.

They took a look at the body and the younger guy turned a little green around the gills. After sending the kid off to direct traffic in case any came along, the sergeant explained apologetically, "He's new. This is probably the first corpse he's ever seen. The first ones are always the hardest."

"Yeah," I added, "and some guys never get used to it."

The sergeant looked at me a little curiously, like he was wondering what the hell I knew about such things, but he didn't ask. Instead, he fished a notebook out of his leather jacket and motioned for me to follow him over into the glare of his patrol car headlights where he could see to write.

He was really pretty good. I've questioned a few people in my day and I know that the kind of cooperation you get depends a lot on your attitude. The sergeant was relaxed and friendly. If he had any suspicions about my role in the accident, they didn't show.

"Okay, Mister . . . ."

"Atkins."

"Okay, Mister Atkins. May I see your drivers' license?"

I slipped the black photostat that said the Great State of California thought I was competent to drive an automobile out of my wallet and passed it over to him.

The sergeant held it up to the light and copied the info into his notebook. Then he looked at it more closely, as if examining the thumbprint affixed to it, and said, "Parker T. Atkins? You aren't the Parker Atkins who gives the news over the radio, are you?"

"We're one and the same, Sergeant."

"How 'bout that!" He sounded genuinely thrilled. "The wife and I listen to you every night at dinner. She'll be real excited when I tell her I met you in person."

"Well, I'm glad to know somebody is listening. Please give her my regards, Sergeant . . . ah . . ."

"Oh. Sorry." He offered his hand. "My name's Framm. Will Framm. It's a real honor to meet you."

We shook and he reassumed his official demeanor. "Okay, Mister Atkins, tell me what you know about all this."

I told him my story and he took copious notes, filling several pages in his little notebook. When I got to the part about the truck driver, the sergeant added, "Yeah, I talked to him when he called in. Said his name was . . . ," Framm flipped back a few pages in his notebook, ". . . Benedetti. Joe Benedetti. Says he saw the Lincoln you said hit the woman. Anything else you can think of that might help us out?"

"No, Sergeant, that's the whole story."

"Alright, Mister Atkins. Ah, one more thing. Would you mind telling me how you happened to be out here at this hour?" With another hint of apology in his voice, he gestured to the notebook with his pencil and added, "Just for the record."

"I wouldn't mind at all. I'm headed home from visiting some friends down in Half Moon Bay."

Sergeant Framm looked up like he was expecting more and I gave him a little shrug. He nodded slightly and I asked, "Any idea who she is?"

"No, I've never seen her before. But from the way she's dressed and everything, I bet it won't be long before someone shows up looking for her."

Turning on my best radio celebrity charm, I said, "Listen, Will, I'd kind of like to follow up on this. Maybe do a story on who killed her and why. Mind if I call you later to find out how the investigation's going?"

"Not at all, Mister Atkins . . . ."

"Call me Park."

He smiled. "Okay, Park. I'd be happy to hear from you any time. And, by the way, keep your eyes open on the way up to The City. There's a white Oldsmobile convertible parked alongside the road, just over the hill there." He gestured up the road to the north. "That might explain how the woman got out here."

"Thanks, Will. You need me for anything else now?"

The sergeant flipped his notebook closed and looked around. "No, I don't think so. I called the coroner before I came out here, so he should be showing up pretty soon. I guess I know where to find you if I think of anymore questions."

"Yup, right on good old KDG every week night at six o'clock sharp."

Sergeant Framm gave me another friendly smile. He shook the hand I offered him and went off to talk to the young deputy who was still standing in the middle of the road with a flashlight and trying not to look at any dead women who happened to be in the vicinity. Will Framm also casually examined both front fenders of my Ford as he walked past them. He was not only good, he was thorough.

The white Oldsmobile was right where Framm said it would be. I found a spot wide enough to pull over on my side of the highway and walked back for a look. The convertible top was down and the brown leather seats were covered with a film of mist. A set of keys dangled from the ignition and the gas gauge needle was pointing to a spot just south of empty. That fact went a long way toward explaining why the dead woman was afoot.

There was one of those license registration certificate holders wrapped around the steering column. I spun the spark wheel on the old brass trench lighter my dad passed on to me as a souvenir of the Great War and read the registration info by its flickering light. The Oldsmobile belonged to one Gladys Doherty who lived at 2315 Buchanan in San Francisco.

Of course, that address meant I'd been wrong about her being one of the rich folks from Nob Hill. Instead, she was one of the rich folks from Pacific Heights, which was almost as far up the social ladder. There were even those who might argue that the Heights were a rung or two higher. I thought about someone who, I was pretty sure, had that opinion and reminded myself to ask her if she knew Gladys Doherty. It seemed likely that she would, since they lived on the same street, about a block apart.

For that matter, I only lived about a dozen blocks from Gladys Doherty's home myself. But in the social scheme of things, those twelve blocks might as well be a million miles because they span the distance between Pacific Heights and the distinctly blue-collar Fillmore District.

Two

In this day and age, you can't think of the telephone as a rich man's luxury anymore. Phones have become a necessity, especially in my line of work. But that doesn't mean the damned things aren't a pain in the butt sometimes. This was one of those times.

I had the telephone at my apartment installed in the kitchen, but it rings plenty loud enough to wake me out of a sound sleep in the bedroom. I looked at my alarm clock through bleary eyes, and when it sunk in that I'd only gotten four hours of sleep so far, I decided whoever wanted to talk to me could wait.

They didn't agree. I'm not one of those people who can't stand not to answer a ringing telephone, but I can't sleep through one, either. When the racket had gone on much longer than it should've taken to convince any reasonable person that nobody was home, I gave up. It took a few more rings for me to stagger down the hall into the kitchen, but the caller persisted. When I finally learned who was on the other end of the line, I wasn't surprised. I only know one person who's that stubborn.

The woman's voice that answered my groggy greeting was unacceptably cheerful. "Good morning, sleepyhead. Aren't you up yet?"

"Hell no, Dandy. I only got to bed a few hours ago."

"Goodness! You must have lost a bundle."

Dandy, known more formally as Danielle Harrison, was referring to the monthly poker game that was my reason for being in Half Moon Bay the night before. She didn't approve.

Actually, it wasn't poker she disliked. An occasional game of cards among gentlemen at a suitable location—say her father's uptown men's club—was tolerable. But poker around the kitchen table with a bunch of Portuguese fishermen I'd befriended while covering a shipwreck story was another matter entirely.

Well, that was just too bad. Since I've been on the wagon, poker and Camel cigarettes are my only remaining vices, and I'm not about to give either of them up, even for the woman in my life.

"No, Dandy. I actually came out ahead for a change."

"That's nice, Park. I'm calling to remind you about the museum luncheon today. You'll have to pick me up in about two hours if we're going to be on time."

I groaned. "Aw, Dandy, I don't know if I can make it. I need to get some sleep."

"Park, you know this is an important event, and my mother is really looking forward to meeting you. Besides, you promised."

Knowing full well that the issue was not a matter she was willing to debate, I sighed and said, "Okay, okay. I'll pick you up at noon."

"Thank you, Parker. Who knows, you might even have a good time!"

Thinking how unlikely that was, I stretched the telephone cord to its limit and turned on the burner under what remained of yesterday morning's coffee. I also remembered the question I needed to ask the love of my life.

"Dandy, before you hang up, I need to ask you something."

"Oh, you can dress casually this afternoon. A suit and tie will be just fine. Maybe your dark blue . . . ."

"No, it's about something else."

"Oh. What, then?"

"Do you happen to know a woman named Gladys Doherty?"

"Know her? Heavens, Park, I grew up with Glady. She lives right down the street."

With all the sensitivity I could muster after only four hours of sleep, I said, "Well then, I'm afraid I've got some bad news for you."

"Oh? What bad news, Park?"

"Your friend Gladys was killed out on Highway One about three o'clock this morning."

I expected tears and cries of dismay, but Dandy simply said, "No, she wasn't."

"Yes, I'm afraid she was. I saw the whole thing. She ran out of gas and was on foot along the highway when a hit-and-run driver got her."

"Park, I don't doubt that you saw someone get hit, but it wasn't Glady. It couldn't have been."

Trying hard not to sound exasperated, I patiently asked, "Why couldn't it have been?"

"Because Glady was with us at the Children's Home Benefit Ball last night until well after two a.m. I know, because I gave her a ride home."

It was slowly dawning on me that I'd jumped to an erroneous conclusion. If Dandy was sure about the time she took Gladys Doherty home, this was clearly a case of mistaken identity. But if the dead woman wasn't Gladys, who the hell was she?

Dandy interrupted my very logical reconstruction of the facts with a very reasonable question. "Park, what made you so sure it was Glady who was killed?"

"The cops found a white Oldsmobile convertible up the road a ways. The car was registered to Gladys Doherty. I just assumed . . . ."

"Tell me, what did the dead woman look like?"

My memory flashed a harsh, headlight-lit image of the woman sprawled against the rocks in her bloody white dress. "She, ah...she looked to be about twenty-five or thirty. She had hazel eyes and . . . ."

"Wait a minute, Park. Was she wearing a white silk jersey evening dress and a diamond teardrop pendant?"

"As a matter of fact, yes. I mean, I don't know if it was silk . . . ."

"Oh, my God! That's Glady's sister, Elaine!"

"But, how do you know . . . ."

"I have to hang up, Park. I need to call Glady right away. She must be devastated! I'll see you at noon. Bye, darling."

"Wait a minute!"

The telephone clicked loudly in my ear as Dandy broke the connection. Grumbling, I hung up and poured some lukewarm stale coffee in an almost clean cup.

Plopping down on the only uncluttered chair at my kitchen table, I wondered how Dandy had known what Elaine Doherty was wearing the night before. Had she seen the woman earlier in the evening? With Dandy, you never knew.

Actually, there were a lot of things one never knew with Dandy. For example, what did a wealthy young society dish like her see in a barely reformed drunk like me? Good question. I'm about eight years older than she and you could hardly say my current career as a news reporter was flourishing when a one-lung station like KDG was the only outfit in town that would hire me.

I'll admit that not knowing why the beautiful and popular Danielle Harrison was so smitten with the ne'er-do-well Parker T. Atkins made me more than a little nervous. But smitten she appeared to be.

We met at a Press Club social function almost a year ago. Dandy was there because she writes for the Chronicle. Her column appears daily in the society section under the overly cute title, "It's Just Dandy!" I was there because KDG needed a news reporter so badly they were willing to take a chance on the former Los Angeles cop-turned-crime reporter who was canned by the L. A. Times for insubordination, incompetence and, mostly, intoxication.

At any rate, Dandy and I hit it off pretty well. I liked her because she was cute and spunky. Who knows why she liked me. Then one thing led to another, and before either of us knew what was happening, we were an item. That's when things started getting serious, and I started getting nervous.

It's not that I don't fancy the idea of Dandy sleeping in my bed on a regular and legal basis, but I'm just not in her league, and I can't see a marriage between us surviving my inability to mix with the swells who inhabit her world. It just wouldn't work, and why she thinks it would is a mystery to me.

But my life is full of mysteries, so one more or less really doesn't make much difference. I just sort of pick one to solve from time to time and it keeps me out of trouble. The mystery I was currently most anxious to unravel concerned the murder of Gladys—no, make that Elaine—Doherty.

My interest in the case was both personal and professional. As a reporter, I knew that Miss Doherty's death had all the elements of a sensational news story. As a guy who witnessed her violent death, I wanted to see Elaine Doherty's killer punished appropriately. Execution by flogging would do nicely.

I debated about calling Sergeant Will Framm to tell him who the unidentified woman might be, but he most likely had that info already. One call to the Dohertys would have revealed the fact that it was Elaine, not Gladys, who was missing. It made more sense to call the sergeant Monday morning—after I found out a little more about the family from Dandy. It never hurts to have a little something to trade when you go fishing for facts from the cops.

Another swallow of the cold brown goop in my cup convinced me I should get moving so there'd be time to stop by Schindler's for a cup of decent coffee and, maybe, some breakfast to go with it. That motivation got me going, and it took no more than thirty minutes to shower, shave and shine. It was exactly eleven when I walked out of the Alta Apartments' foyer and turned left on McAllister.

Schindler's is a popular kosher dining room in a predominantly Jewish neighborhood, so you'd expect the food to be good. It was. Mama Schindler made sure of that by overseeing the kitchen personally.

Two-and-a-half blocks later, at the corner of Golden Gate and Webster, I walked under the sidewalk awning and into the small Victorian-style building that houses Schindler's. Mister Schindler greeted me at the door, dressed as he always was, in a white shirt and black bow tie. He was a big man and bald as a billiard ball, with a booming voice that let everyone in the place know that their favorite radio news broadcaster was favoring them with his presence.

Mr. Schindler seated me at a small table next to a window that overlooked the sidewalk, and I perused the neatly hand-lettered menu. For me, personally, the only drawback to Schindler's was the fact that there was no bacon or ham to go with my eggs and bagel. This was a major sacrifice, but one I was usually willing to make in exchange for a slab of the most tender beefsteak you ever ate. The steak, however, was out of the question this morning. I had to leave room for the soggy little crustless sandwiches and minuscule gob of potato salad I was expected to enjoy at Dandy's luncheon.

The eggs, as usual, were delicious and my bagel was toasted to perfection. After dallying long enough to savor a second cup of Schindler's rich coffee, I paid the tab with a quarter and a dime, left another dime on the table for the great service, and hot-footed it back home.

The Ford was parked across the street from my apartment, and as I approached it, I wished there'd been time to wash the darn thing. Parking a lowly three-year-old Ford among the fancy new Packards, Lincolns and Cadillacs in the museum lot was bad enough. Parking a dirty Ford there was really poor form. But what the hell, I don't have a chauffeur, either.

Three

My usual route to Dandy's—out Steiner to Alta Plaza Park, then east on Clay to Buchanan—took me past the Doherty home. Twenty-three-fifteen was on the west side of Buchanan, and it was a typical Pacific Heights residence—a large three-story Victorian displaying the requisite collection of gables and gingerbread.

Beyond their low wrought iron fence, the Dohertys' circular drive was surrounded by a lawn that was exactly the correct shade of green. The drive was crowded with several big sedans, including one with a liveried chauffeur lounging against its fender. Well, there's nothing like a death in the family to bring out the relatives.

This was obviously not a good time to pay a call on the grieving parents and sister of the deceased, especially since I was only about two minutes away from being late to pick up Dandy. My determination to learn who killed Elaine Doherty and why could wait until tomorrow.

Pulling away from the curb, I wondered if at least some of that determination wasn't just because I was still a crime reporter at heart, and like an old bloodhound, I missed the excitement of being on the scent of a big story.

Dandy's place—technically, her parents' place—was pretty much a carbon copy of the Doherty home except it was on the opposite side of the street and the gingerbread looked a little different. As I pulled up the drive, one of the ornate double entry doors flew open and Dandy trotted down the front steps.

I watched her and sighed a little because Dandy is one of those women who make men do things like that. Today her slender frame was draped in a cheery little yellow dress that swirled around her to a point just below the knees. This was accompanied by white gloves, white shoes with heels of a moderate height, and a yellow straw fedora, which was cocked at a jaunty angle atop her short, permanently-waved, dark brown hair.

She was halfway down the steps by the time I stopped staring and started getting out of the car. Before I could get any further, Dandy called out, "Don't bother, Park. I can get the door."

After hopping nimbly onto the passenger end of the seat, she slid over and gave me an affectionate kiss square on the mouth. No little pecks on the cheek for this girl. No, sir. As I slipped the transmission into low, Dandy used the handkerchief from my breast pocket to wipe away some remnants of lipstick from my mouth and said, "Thanks for being on time, darling. I know this sort of thing bores you to tears, and I appreciate that you're letting me drag you along."

I looked at Dandy and the sincerity that sparkled back at me from her big brown eyes drove the smart-Alec remark I'd been about to make right out of my head. Left with nothing else to say, I just smiled and turned my attention to the task of getting us to the Palace of the Legion of Honor.

We were heading west on Clement Street and Dandy was busy enlightening me as to which big shots I was likely to encounter at the benefit luncheon, when I subtly changed the subject to one in which I had a good deal more interest. "Dandy, did you get to talk to Gladys Doherty?"

"Only for a moment. Glady was awfully upset. I told her I would stop in again tomorrow."

Dandy came up with my next question before I did. "You're wondering how I knew what Elaine was wearing last night, aren't you?"

"Yes, I sort of was."

"Well, I'd like you to think I have mystical psychic powers, but the truth is Elaine was at the ball for a few minutes last night, and I remembered how she was dressed. And when you told me the accident victim was driving Glady's car, I knew it had to be Elaine because that's why she stopped by . . . to borrow Glady's car."

"What time was all of this?"

"Gosh, Park, I'm not sure. She was only there for a little while. I remember Glady and I were hitting dear old Missus Hillier up for a sizeable donation when Elaine came over and took Glady away. I didn't see either of them for a little while, and then Glady showed up again and apologized for deserting me. Oh, and that's when she asked if I could give her a ride home because Elaine had taken her car."

"Try to pin down the time you saw Elaine, honey. It's important."

After a few moments of quiet contemplation, Dandy said, "The best I can do is say that it was sometime before ten o'clock. That's when we drew the raffle winners and I know Elaine came in before that."

"What sort of mood was she in? I mean, did she behave normally?"

"I didn't notice anything special about her, except that she was in a hurry to see Glady and the way she interrupted us was a little rude."

"What about Gladys? How was she after they talked?"

"Glady's kind of wacky to begin with, so it's hard to say, but she seemed normal. She didn't act depressed or anything, if that's what you're getting at."

I was mentally sorting out the questions I still wanted to ask, when Dandy's curiosity got the better of her. "What's this all about, Park? What makes you so interested in Glady and Elaine?"

I decided to give it to her straight. Dandy was a big girl—she could handle it. "I'm interested because Elaine's death wasn't an accident."

"What do you mean? You said she was run over by a hit-and-run driver."

"That's true, but there's more. I saw it happen. The driver went out of his way to hit her. Elaine Doherty was murdered."

"Murdered? For heaven's sake! Who would want to murder Elaine?"

"That's what I'm trying to find out. Have either of the Doherty girls ever been in trouble? Any scandals? Anything like that?"

"Scandals? The Doherty sisters? Park, you must be joking."

"Oh, come on, Dandy. Even the high and mighty of Pacific Heights step in a little manure now and then. You said Gladys is a little wacky. How wacky is she?"

"I only meant she's impulsive. Glady likes to clown around. She just gets carried away sometimes."

"How carried away? Does she drink?"

"Of course she drinks. Everybody drinks!"

I glanced at Dandy just as she realized what she'd said. "Oh, Park, I'm sorry. I didn't mean . . . I wasn't thinking."

"That's alright. Forget it. Tell me about the Doherty family. Where do they fit into the social scheme of things around here?"

Dandy was looking at me, probably trying to decide if she needed to make more of her apology. I was relieved that she decided to drop it and get back to the Dohertys.

"They're one of the most prominent families in San Francisco. They own Pacific Eastern Shipping. Glady's granddad came out here sometime during the eighteen-nineties and built the company up from nothing into a worldwide shipping concern. Both Elaine and Glady had the very best upbringing. They've been to the most prestigious schools and . . . ."

"A couple of spoiled brats, huh?"

"Park! I know you think my friends are a bunch of stuffed shirts, but you're wrong about the Doherty sisters. Glady is one of my best friends. I would know if either she or Elaine had ever been in any kind of trouble, and they haven't."

The fervor of Dandy's tone made me look at her as I turned right off of Clement into Lincoln Park. I'd always thought Dandy was a pretty good judge of character, but she was missing something this time. She had to be. Little rich girls who've never been in trouble don't get murdered out on lonely roads in the middle of the night by big guys in Lincolns.

More important at the moment, however, was the irritation showing on Dandy's face. In my usual, inimitable style, I'd upset her with my spoiled brat remark, and under the circumstances, it seemed like a good idea to set things right again before we arrived at our destination.

"I'm sorry, honey. What I saw last night disturbed me, and I need to find some answers. I didn't mean to push so hard."

"It's okay, Park. I understand. It's just that when you belittle my friends, I feel like you're criticizing me, too. Can you see that?"

I nodded and she took my hand and held onto it as we wound our way up through the evergreens of Lincoln Park golf course. A moment later we crested the hill and there it was: A grand monument to the world's great art, the Palace of the Legion of Honor.

Valets were on hand to park the automobiles of those who didn't have a chauffeur to take care of such trivialities. One of the maroon-jacketed young men opened Dandy's door and helped her out, while another handed me a brass claim token, being careful not to brush up against the Ford lest he soil his pretty jacket.

We walked into the Palace's grand forecourt and past the full-sized replica of Rodin's Thinker. At the top of the steps I caught a glimpse of our reflections in the large glass entry doors. In that brief moment I saw us as others did and felt my chest swell with pride at the beauty of the woman on my arm. Just before we reached the doors, I ushered Dandy to one side.

Before she could ask what was wrong, I said, "Dandy, I forgot to tell you something important."

I said it in a solemn tone and she looked up into my eyes with concern. "What, Park?"

"You look absolutely beautiful today!"

A sly little grin twitched at the corners of her mouth. "Why, Park, thank you. But you didn't need to say that. I already knew you'd noticed."

"Is that so? And just how did you know that?"

Dandy learned forward on tiptoes and whispered in my ear, "I saw you looking at me when I came down the steps at home. The expression on your face told me all I needed to know."

With that, I got a socially acceptable kiss on the cheek and she took my arm again, turning me toward the museum entrance. I breathed deeply and marched bravely into the fray.

The luncheon was almost exactly what I expected it to be. Dandy's mother, however, was not. I'd anticipated a typical looking-down-her-nose society matron, and while Samantha Harrison certainly looked the part, she had a twinkle in her eye that immediately told me different.

The first words out of her mouth were, "So you're the rascal who's gotten my daughter in such a dither. It's about time you came forward and let us have a look at you."

With Dandy clinging to my arm and beaming up at me, I said, "I'm honored to meet you, Missus Harrison. And, having met you, I now see very clearly where Danielle gets her beauty."

Samantha Harrison looked me square in the eye for a very long time, and just when my most sincere expression was about to crumble, I saw the same sly little grin begin to twitch at the corners of her mouth. She turned to Dandy and said, "Very well, Danielle, you may keep him, but you be careful. It would seem your Mister Atkins is a charmer."

I spent most of the next two hours standing around inconspicuously in convenient corners of various ornate galleries while Dandy did her job. At long last, when she was through socializing and gathering material for her column, Dandy sought me out in my current corner and granted the reprieve I'd been more or less patiently awaiting.

We retrieved the Ford and started out of Lincoln Park to the north, via the El Camino Del Mar. On the way, I pulled over on the narrow shoulder for a few minutes so we could look down on the gleaming new bridge that now spanned the Golden Gate. Its vivid orange stood out in sharp contrast to the bright blues of sky and bay. A handful of puffy little clouds scudded above our panorama, mirroring the dazzling white of several dozen sails dotting the water.

Our next stop was Baker Beach. Even though the afternoon air was beginning to cool, Dandy couldn't resist taking a walk on such a beautiful day. We wandered among the eucalyptus and pines that dotted the cliffs above the beach, with frequent stops to stare off across the water toward the rugged Marin headlands. The kisses that punctuated each of these pauses gradually grew longer and more intense until we decided it was a little too chilly to walk any further.

We picked up dinner--a block of Swiss cheese, some coleslaw and a freshly baked loaf of rye--at Goldenrath's Delicatessen and headed for my apartment. There we dined to the accompaniment of Harry Owens' radio program, directly from Hawaii over KROW. When Harry and Hilo Hattie signed off, I turned the dial around to KDG, where a program of romantic recorded music replaced The News With Parker T. Atkins on weekends.

Leaning back on the couch with Dandy nestled under my right arm, I began what I was pretty sure would be the evening's last conversation that amounted to more than a word or two. "Dandy, what time are you going to see Gladys tomorrow?"

She turned her head far enough to look me in the eye and said, "I thought I'd run over and see her a little after lunch. Why? You aren't trying to wrangle an invitation to visit a spoiled brat, are you?"

"Touché. But I really need to ask her some questions about last night, and since you're going to see her anyway, I thought maybe . . . ."

"Park, you're incorrigible! The girl just lost her sister!"

I sighed, "I know, honey, but I've got to get an angle on this thing."

Dandy looked up at my hopeful expression and gave in. "Oh, alright. Just promise me you'll be tactful. Please?"

"Honey, I promise to be the very essence of tact from this moment on."

That matter resolved, we picked up where we'd left off at Baker Beach. When our kisses reached an intensity that was well beyond the point of no return, I led Dandy into the bedroom and very tactfully removed her pretty yellow dress.

Four

6:00 a.m.—Monday—June 7, 1937

Residents of the Fillmore District may not live in Victorian mansions or look out on great views of the bay, but we do have the best smelling mornings in town. Within a block-and-a-half of my apartment there are three bakeries, including the big Langendorf Company which delivers its bread all over the city.

So when my alarm clock began clanging at six on Monday morning, I awoke to the usual delicious smells of fresh bread, Danish and donuts. And those delightful aromas were frosted with sweet memories from the night before. Dandy and I have always pleased each other in bed, but this was one of those special times when our passions soared higher and farther than either of us expected. Afterwards, we lay there for a very long time, her face nestled against my neck and my hand on the warm velvet of her back.

When I finally delivered Dandy back to her parents' house around ten, we shared a long intense goodnight kiss on the porch and she sighed, "Golly, Park, wouldn't it be wonderful if we could just say goodnight in our own bed instead of ending our evenings like this?"

Those words rang through my dreams all night. They were still there when I woke up and I knew if I didn't make them go away, their bittersweet message would haunt me for days. So as I showered and got dressed for work, I systematically erased them by reminding myself of all the reasons why Dandy and I could never marry. By the time I walked through the foyer and out to my car, I'd successfully driven her words from my mind. Most of the exhilaration I'd felt when I woke up went with them.

The offices and studios of radio station KDG are located on the fourth floor of the Owl Drug Building at Third and Market. From a news standpoint it's an ideal location, being across the street from the San Francisco Examiner and only a couple of blocks from the Chronicle.

I share a small, but humble office at KDG with my assistant, Miss Charlene Blanchard. Together, Charlie and I comprise the station's entire news department. Essentially, she assembles the bulk of each day's half hour news broadcast while I concentrate on digging into a big story or two. Fortunately for both KDG and me, Charlie is very, very competent.

She's also very dedicated. Sadly, Charlie's dedication is due to the fact that she has no life outside of the station. I think that's because, physically, Charlie can only be described as a plain person. She has a plain, ordinary face and a plain, ordinary body. Her hair is plain and she wears plain clothes. In fact, the only reason for anybody of either sex to pay the slightest bit of attention to Charlene Blanchard is because she is very good at what she does. With that for motivation, Charlie puts her entire heart and soul into her work.

"Good morning, Park. Have a good weekend?"

"It had its moments. How 'bout you? Do anything exciting?"

"Are you kidding?"

I let the small talk end there and flopped into the squeaky old wooden swivel chair behind my desk. Charlie's desk, which is jammed up against mine so we sit face to face, was piled high with morning editions of the Examiner, Chronicle, Call Bulletin, and Oakland Tribune. She'd obviously been there for a while because several pages of the legal pad she uses to make notes on the day's top stories were already filled.

Gesturing toward the stack of newspapers, I asked, "What's going on in the world this morning?"

Charlie flipped back through her notes and read me the highlights. "The U.A.W. says they reached an agreement with Ford last night and the Richmond plant strike ends today. The C.I.O. Steel Workers sent a telegram to Roosevelt this morning asking him to intervene in their Ohio strike. Some school principal down in Santa Cruz—a guy named Reuel L. Fick—has been arrested for lewd and lascivious conduct with twelve-year-old girls. And, let's see . . . the traffic count on the Golden Gate Bridge is up to two-hundred-thousand cars for the nine days since it opened.

"Oh, and they finally found that Western Air Express plane. The one that went down last December? It crashed into a mountain in Utah, twenty feet from the peak. Can you beat that? If the plane had been twenty feet higher, they would have made it. The Chron ran a big front-page sidebar, complete with a photo, telling how the plane's hostess had just turned down two marriage proposals before the crash. The headline says, 'She Gave Up Marriage For Death.'

"Anyway, those are the biggest stories. What are you going to work on? One of these, or have you got something else in mind?"

"I've got something else, Charlie, but it's going to take a few days to dig it all out. We'll start the story off tonight as a special crime report and continue it for the next couple of days. So just leave me about two minutes out of tonight's broadcast."

"What's the story? You get a line on something hot?"

"It has to do with a society gal named Elaine Doherty who was killed out on Highway One Saturday night."

"Hey, that rings a bell. I think the Call gave it about an inch-and-a-half somewhere around page ten. They called it a hit-and-run accident. You know something they don't?"

"Yeah, I saw it happen and it wasn't any accident."

"Really? What makes you say that?"

I spent the next couple of minutes filling Charlie in on what I knew about Elaine Doherty's murder so far. She wasn't impressed.

"Are you sure this is really a big mystery? I mean, maybe the guy was just drunk or something. If you cover this thing as a special crime report and it turns out to be nothing, you'll end up with egg all over your face."

I told Charlie not to worry about it. After all, it was my face. She gave me one last disapproving look and went off to check the United Press Wire Service teletype. I picked up the phone and put in a long-distance call to Deputy Will Framm at the San Mateo County Sheriff's San Bruno substation.

"Framm here."

"Good morning, Will. This is Park Atkins. Thought I'd check in and see what you had so far on that hit-and-run Saturday night."

"Oh, hi, Park. I'm afraid I haven't got much. All we know at this point is the victim's identity. Traced it down from that Oldsmobile parked out there. It's registered to a Gladys Doherty at an address up there in The City. But her sister was driving the car . . . Elaine Doherty, age twenty-nine."

"I tried talking to the family, but I didn't get anywhere. Once they knew what happened, it was hopeless. I'll try to get up there this afternoon and fill in some of the blanks."

Actually, I was pleased that Framm wasn't any farther along with his investigation. It gave me a chance to toss a little information his way in exchange for future cooperation. I told him about Elaine showing up at the Children's Benefit sometime before ten to borrow her sister's car and I passed along what I'd learned about the family from Dandy.

"Hell, you've been busy. How'd you come up with all that so quick?"

"Mostly by coincidence. Turns out a close friend of mine knows the younger sister pretty well. She saw Elaine at the benefit and filled me in on the family."

"I see. Thanks for the help. If you check with me tomorrow, I may have something new from talking to them this afternoon."

"What about the Lincoln? Any chance of tracking it down?"

"Maybe. We've already circulated your description of it and the driver to all the other police departments in the area. And the car should have a pretty good dent in the left front fender, so we're telling the big automobile body repair shops to watch for it. Something may come of that, but the odds of getting a solid lead are pretty slim. There are just too many shops around the Bay. We can't possibly cover them all.

"I also put in a call to the Division of Motor Vehicles up in Sacramento and requested a make and model registration check. If it really was a new Lincoln Zephyr you saw Saturday night and it's registered in California, we might get lucky. That's a pretty high-priced automobile and I don't imagine there's more than a few hundred of them in the state."

That is, I thought, if the car wasn't stolen to begin with. Experience told me the chances of making a connection through Motor Vehicles weren't much better than picking up a lead from the body shops. But you never know.

I thanked Framm for his help and told him I'd check in on Tuesday. I didn't mention that I was planning to see Gladys Doherty before he did. Even though the deputy was being helpful, cops tend to get a little touchy when they think a civilian might be muddying up an investigation.

Next, I added a few more cents to KDG's telephone bill by calling my contact at Lloyds of London. Because San Francisco is a major shipping center, Lloyds maintains an office here. I'd called them before when I needed background on a ship or a shipping company. The man I'd spoken to on those occasions was Ambrose Whithers. Whithers' accent was so thick you could've made a pretty fair gimlet with the lime juice that came dripping over the line.

"Whithers here. Who's calling please?"

"Ambrose, this is Park Atkins at radio station KDG. How are you today?"

"Oh, Mister Atkins. Good to speak with you again. How may I be of service?"

"I need some background on the Pacific Eastern Shipping Lines. What can you tell me about them?"

"Pacific Eastern, you say? They are one of the biggest and the best. Strictly top drawer."

"They've been around for a while, huh?"

"Yes, you might say that. The firm was founded by Jacob Doherty, who is somewhat of a legend in shipping circles. Typical rags-to-riches sort of story. He began with nothing back before the turn of the century and built a very powerful company. I may be able to find some dates and more specific details if those things are of importance to you."

"No, thanks. I don't need that much. Is Jacob Doherty still involved with the company?"

"Oh my, yes. He's quite an old man, but spry and active. His son, Rutherford, is now the titular head of the firm, but I understand Jacob still runs the company . . . with an iron hand, I'm told."

"Has Pacific Eastern run into any difficulties recently? Problems with the longshoremen or anything?"

"Nothing that I am aware of. As far as Lloyds is concerned, Pacific Eastern has a spotless record . . . highest possible rating, and all that."

I thanked Whithers for his help and leaned back in my chair. It squeaked and I wondered what to do next. Background research is a boring job, but it has to be done because you never know when you'll come across some minor detail that fills in a piece of the puzzle.

Picking up the phone a third time, I called Bobby Newmann over at the Chronicle. He runs their morgue and maintains his own clipping files on people in the news. Bobby is always helpful, in spite of the fact that the Chronicle and KDG are competitors of sorts in the news business—though I doubt anybody at the Chron is too awfully worried about whatever advertising revenue they might be losing to KDG.

"Morgue, Newmann."

"Hello, Bobby. Park Atkins."

"Hi, Park. What's going on in the excitin' world of radio these days?"

"Not a whole hell of a lot. Anything new down there in the basement?"

"Naw, the only excitement we get down here is when it rains and the creek rises. Now, if your lady friend would come around once in a while, that might liven things up a little."

I smiled into the phone and said, "I'll talk to Dandy about that. Maybe she can get one of those damned benefit societies to hold a luncheon or something down there."

"Hell, that's all I need. Don't do me any favors, buddy."

"Okay, maybe you can do me one instead."

"Sure, whatcha need?"

"Everything you've got on the Doherty family. Jacob, Rutherford, Elaine, Gladys, and the mother, whatever her name is."

I could hear the suspicion in Bobby's voice as he asked, "What's goin' on with them? You got wind of a scandal or somethin'?"

"No, nothing like that. The family's oldest daughter was killed in an automobile accident Saturday night. I'm doing a piece on it and I need some background."

"Yeah? Since when are you covering the society beat?"

"I'm not. It was a hit-and-run. Thought I'd do a little preaching about highway safety."

Not sounding entirely convinced, Bobby said, "Okay. I'll see what I've got. Stop by tomorrow morning. Hey, and bring a bag of those macaroon tarts from Schubert's with ya. I don't provide all this great service for free, ya know."

I promised to bring the tarts and thanked Bobby in advance for his help. As I dropped the telephone handset back onto its cradle, the office door opened and no less than KDG's owner and general manager, William L. Kastner, bustled in. Or it might have been Porky the Pig. Sometimes it's hard to tell them apart.

Towering over his short, roly-poly frame by nearly a foot, I stood to shake hands and Kastner said, "Hello, Parker. Sit down, sit down. Don't let me interrupt. Just hadn't been in to visit with you for a while. Wanted to see how things are going."

That was a lie. Kastner made it a point to stick his chubby little cheeks into our office at least once a week to check up on me. But I really didn't blame him, given my track record. Kastner just wanted to be sure I was still sober and earning my keep. He sure as hell didn't need a drunken news broadcaster getting him in Dutch with the Federal Communications Commission.

I smiled back and said, "Things are just great, Mister Kastner. Could use a little oil for the squeak in my chair, there, but other than that . . . ."

"Glad to hear it, Parker. Glad to hear it. By the way, I got a nice compliment on you at a luncheon with the mayor the other day. Seems he's a big fan of yours. Says he never misses your broadcast. He especially liked your coverage of the bridge opening. Just thought you might like to know that. Well, keep up the good work, Parker. See you next time."

I said, "Bye. Thanks for stopping in," to the door as it slammed shut behind Kastner's fat butt. Well, I guess I couldn't blame him for being abrupt, either. These little employee morale talks probably take a lot of time out of his busy luncheon schedule. And as far as the mayor was concerned, he ought to be pleased with my coverage. His press secretary wrote it. Oh well, just so long as everybody's happy.

When Charlie returned with a handful of yellow teletype paper torn off the wire service machine, she peeked through the door cautiously before entering.

I put her mind at ease. "The coast is clear. He's gone."

Charlie demonstrated her most attractive feature—a sheepish grin that always makes me think of Stan Laurel—and said, "I didn't want to interrupt if you and Mister Kastner were in conference."

"Come on, Charlie, you know better than that. A conference almost always takes more than the thirty seconds Kastner allots us for his weekly visit. He just stopped by to make sure we weren't having a drunken orgy in here."

She looked a little longingly, like maybe a drunken orgy wouldn't be all that bad, and slipped into her chair. Using a wooden ruler for a straight edge to tear against, Charlie began ripping the U.P. wire service copy into story-sized pieces. Noting that most of the five or six feet of yellow paper went directly into her wastebasket, I said, "Nothing new on the wire, huh?"

"No. Just more on the steel strike." She paused, quickly scanning a story that U.P. thought was only worth about two inches of teletype. "Amelia Earhart is en route from Brazil to Africa on her round-the-world flight. You want to throw that in tonight?"

"Only if she doesn't make it."

"Parker!"

"Sorry. Just kidding."

The rest of the morning went about the same. Charlie was efficiently assembling and writing the evening's broadcast while I fiddled around at being a crime reporter with damn little to show for the effort.

By eleven-thirty I was spending more time looking at my wristwatch than anything else. It was a toss-up as to which I was looking forward to the most—interviewing Gladys Doherty or seeing Dandy. I finally gave up and dialed Douglas one-four-one-four for the second time that morning. The Chronicle's switchboard put me right through to the Society Department.

"Hello. Dandy Harrison here."

My chair screeched as I turned toward the wall to gain a little privacy. "Hi Dandy, it's me."

"Hi, darling. How's the most fantastic lover in the whole world this morning?"

"That's what I was calling to find out. How are you?"

"Why, Park! I'm blushing."

"Good, you should be. Are we still on to see Gladys this afternoon?"

"Uh-huh. I just talked to her. She's expecting us about one."

"Great. Will you be ready to go pretty soon?"

"Why, darling, it isn't even noon yet."

"I know. I just thought if we left early we'd have time to stop somewhere for lunch."

"I was hoping you'd think of that. I'll be downstairs in ten minutes."

Charlie was staring at me sort of absently when I squeaked around to hang up the telephone. Feeling a trifle embarrassed, I said, "Didn't anyone ever tell you it's impolite to listen in on other people's conversations?"

She jumped a little, realizing what she'd been doing and that she'd been caught at it. "I'm sorry, Park. I didn't mean to . . . ."

"Don't worry about it, kiddo. It's all a mystery to me, too."

Five

I picked Dandy up in front of the Chronicle plant on Mission at Fifth and we zigzagged our way through traffic over to Market, then out Grant to Vallejo Street. Our destination was the New Pisa restaurant a block from Washington Square in the heart of Little Italy.

We ordered the forty-cent lunch special: Soup, pasta, choice of entree, coffee, and homemade cookies. Dandy had a glass of wine with her kidney stew. I stuck to coffee and scaloppini.

While we ate, I reported on my morning's efforts—the call to Deputy Framm and my other inquiries. I also mentioned Kastner's visit. That was a mistake. It irritated the hell out of Dandy.

"Why doesn't that pompous ass just leave you alone and let you do your job?"

"Kastner's just protecting his investment. He took a hell of a chance hiring me in the first place. Nobody else wanted a broken-down drunk around."

"Oh, Park, that is a bunch of baloney! Kastner saw an opportunity to get one of the best reporters in the business for peanuts and he grabbed it. Your news program is the only thing that keeps KDG afloat and Kastner knows it. He's the one who should be grateful, not you. Besides, you've changed. You work hard and you don't drink anymore."

"Dandy, we've talked about this before. When the hell are you gonna get it through that thick head of yours that alcoholism isn't like influenza? There is no cure. You don't get over it. All the things that made me a drunk to begin with are still inside me. I'll have to fight them for the rest of my damned life!"

I watched the tears filling Dandy's soft brown eyes and hated myself. My frustration with our situation had gotten the better of me and I'd taken it out on her.

Dandy dabbed at her eyes with a hanky and I reached across the red-and-white-checkered tablecloth to take her hand. "Honey, I'm sorry. I didn't mean to hurt you, I just . . . ."

Her voice was quiet and husky. "It's alright, Park. I understand." She looked at me for a few seconds, and then shook her head as the dam inside her burst. "No, damn it! I don't! I don't understand any of this!"

Suddenly, she was out of her chair and walking briskly toward the powder room while everyone else in the place glared at the heel who'd made the pretty lady cry. I sat back and lit a cigarette. To hell with 'em. To hell with the whole damned world.

Two Camels later, Dandy returned looking very composed and under control. But she didn't sit down. She just walked up to the table and said, "It's getting late, Park. We'd better go."

We rode across town in silence and I didn't do a damned thing about it. Instead I made up my mind to end our hopeless romance before I hurt Dandy anymore than I already had. She was a sweet, loving kid and she sure as hell deserved better than Park Atkins.

The Doherty place looked just about like it had the day before, except there was only one car in the driveway today. That car, however, was a surprise. The last time I saw Gladys' white Oldsmobile it was parked out on Highway One. I wondered why it was here instead of at the Sheriff's impound lot. I also wondered if anybody had bothered to look it over. If they hadn't, Will Framm wasn't half the cop I thought he was.

The mansion's interior was just what the outside promised it would be. The Dohertys' houseman admitted us into a craftsman's paradise of carved woods, opulent fabrics, and enough stained glass to outfit a cathedral. The treatment Dandy received, however, was a little more formal than I would have expected in the home of an old friend. Miss Gladys was expecting her and requested that we wait in the library.

So we waited in the library. The room was large with a high ceiling, tall windows, an ornate fireplace, and mahogany paneling. There were some comfy-looking chairs, a couple of smoking stands, and an end table or two scattered around on the reddish-brown oriental carpet. A desk with a telephone was placed diagonally in one corner next to a window. To my surprise, the library also contained books—hundreds of them lining floor-to-ceiling shelves on either side of the fireplace. Some of the books even looked like they might have been read once upon a time. Since Dandy and I still didn't have anything to say to each other, I busied myself thumbing through an illustrated edition of Hans Christian Anderson.

When Gladys finally slipped in through one of the eight-foot, hand-carved double doors, she and Dandy greeted each other like long lost sisters. The two of them together made an interesting contrast. Where Dandy was dark-haired and petite, Gladys Doherty was fair, blonde and big-boned. She wasn't chubby by any means; there was just a lot of girl there.

After hugs and sympathy from Dandy, Gladys looked up and noticed me standing there. Dandy made the formal introduction.

"Glady, this is my friend, Parker Atkins."

The way Dandy said the word "friend" stung a little, but Glady was delighted to see me. At least, that's what she said. I said, "Nice to meet you, Gladys. I'm very sorry about your sister."

She looked at me as though she actually appreciated my condolences. "Thank you, Parker. Her death has hit everyone in the family pretty hard."

Dandy explained my presence by saying, "Glady, I didn't tell you this before, but Park . . . well, he was there when Elaine was killed."

That was a shock, and Gladys jerked around to stare at me in horror. She stammered, "You . . . you were out there . . . on . . . on the coast road Saturday night?"

I nodded.

"Did . . . did you see Elaine get . . . I mean, did you see the accident?"

I nodded again and Dandy continued her explanation, "You see, Glady, Park has some suspicions about Elaine's death. He doesn't believe it was an accident and . . . well, he wants to find out for sure. To do that, he needs to ask you some questions."

Gladys Doherty was still staring at me, studying my face intently. When Dandy finished, Gladys turned and walked slowly toward the fireplace. Absently, she explored the colorful glass shade of a Tiffany lamp with her fingers and asked, "What makes you think Elaine's death wasn't an accident?"

"Two things. First, when I saw Elaine, she was on foot in the middle of the highway."

Gladys looked up quickly. "The Sheriff's deputy said my car was out of gas, so it makes sense that she was walking. Elaine was probably just trying to find someone who would help her get some gas."

"Yes, but Elaine wasn't walking. She was running . . . running for all she was worth, as if someone were chasing her."

Gladys nodded in a way that made me think of a small child who was only admitting the truth because there was no other way out. I continued, "The other reason I know it wasn't an accident is that I saw the car swerve out of its way to hit Elaine."

She looked up at me again. This time there was a trace of anger in both her expression and her words. "How can you possibly know that? Maybe the driver was drunk and didn't know what he was doing. Did you ever consider that?"

"Yes, as a matter of fact, my assistant suggested the same thing this morning. The trouble is, I got a good look at the driver when he passed me. The man showed no signs of being drunk. He was alert and concentrating on the road. His driving wasn't at all erratic until he swerved to hit Elaine."

She moved around the room a little aimlessly, shaking her head, as if denying any possibility that her sister could have been murdered. Dandy, bless her heart, stepped in and tried to make things easier.

"Glady, I know it must be hard to accept that somebody deliberately killed Elaine, but Park saw what he saw. All he wants to do is find out why Elaine died. Would you try to answer his questions?"

Gladys stopped shaking her head and shrugged. "Alright. There's no reason on this earth why anyone would want to kill Elaine, but I'll answer your questions, if I can."

I smiled a thank-you at Dandy, but she didn't seem to notice. So I sighed a little and asked the first question that came to mind.

"Dandy says Elaine stopped by the charity benefit Saturday night to talk to you. What did she want to talk about?"

Her answer came quickly, if a little belligerently. "That's easy. She wanted to borrow my car. Hers wasn't working right."

"If she didn't have a car, how did she get to the benefit?"

"I don't know. Maybe Daddy dropped her off on his way to a meeting or something."

"Did she say why she needed a car? Where she wanted to go?"

"Elaine just said it was a nice evening and she wanted to go for a drive. That's all."

In a pig's eye, that was all. Dandy told me Elaine was in such a hurry she interrupted Gladys in the middle of a conversation, so there had to be something more to it than just needing a car to take a drive. And, more to the point, why was Gladys lying about it? I decided to try a different tack.

"Gladys, was Elaine seeing anybody on a regular basis, like a serious boyfriend?"

Again, the answer came quickly. "No. Elaine didn't have anybody like that." She thought about it for a moment and must have decided I was getting a poor impression of her sister because she added, "I don't mean that Elaine wasn't popular. She had lots of friends. She was on everybody's guest list."

"Then she went to a lot of parties and events?"

Gladys was obviously more comfortable with questions about her sister's social life. "Oh my, yes. Elaine was always busy. Hardly an evening went by that she didn't attend at least one function. Some nights, she went to two or three. Her weekends were always jam-packed."

"Then I wonder why Elaine didn't have anything better to do Saturday night than go for a drive. The way she was dressed, I thought maybe she'd been to a party or something."

Gradually, Gladys realized I'd trapped her. That realization arrived in the middle of another concocted explanation.

"Now that you mention it, I think Elaine did say she might stop by the Winslows'. They were hosting some sort of a party that night and . . . ." Abruptly, she put on a tragic expression and turned to Dandy. On the verge of tears, Gladys said, "I'm sorry. You'll have to forgive me, but I can't go on with this. Maybe some other time . . . ."

Dandy embraced Gladys and looked at me with raised eyebrows over the girl's shoulder. I nodded and she said, "That's alright, darling. We know you're upset. Park understands how difficult this is for you."

On cue, I chimed in, "Yes, of course. I'm sorry my questions upset you. We'll be going now. I need to get back to the station anyway. I've got a news broadcast to prepare."

It was so obvious you could almost hear the click in her brain as Gladys made the connection between all my questions and what I did for a living. The expression on her face when she turned around was one of impending doom.

Her words came slowly. "You . . . you aren't going to talk about Elaine on the radio are you? You aren't going to say she was murdered?"

"Well," I shrugged, "I do a news program and Elaine's death is news."

She panicked. "No! You can't! Promise me you won't! That would be terrible!"

Gladys might have been upset because she feared a scandal, but I had the definite feeling this was something more than that. She was literally in a state of terror. Being the rat that I am, I pushed her a little harder to see what would happen.

"I'm sorry, Gladys, but I saw your sister being murdered and I have to report it that way. Besides, if we get the public involved, someone may come forward with something that will help us find Elaine's killer."

The big blonde's eyes were wide as hubcaps. She groaned, "Oh, God," and ran from the room, sobbing hysterically. Dandy glared at me like I'd sprouted horns and a forked tail. Her look hurt, but she and I were through anyway, so it really didn't make that much difference. Like hell.

We let ourselves out, and on the way to my car, I stopped to look at the Oldsmobile. The top was still down and I could see most of the interior from where I stood. It was clean as a whistle. Maybe Framm's people had looked it over after all.

Being a two-door, the car had one of those front seats that's hinged so the back folds forward to let passengers into the rear. The space between the bottom and back cushions on seats like that serves as a handy repository for all the little things that fall out of pockets or purses and disappear. Just for the hell of it, I pushed the seat back forward. The small pink ticket stub between the cushions told me that if Framm's people had examined the Olds, they weren't very thorough.

I resisted the temptation to take the ticket with me because that would be concealing evidence and interfering with a police investigation. I did, however, take a good look at it. Someone who'd been in the Oldsmobile had also been to the Rose Bowl Dance Pavilion in Larkspur on the evening of June fifth, the night Elaine Doherty died.

There was a lot more silence between Dandy and me on our way back to her office. I'd at least expected her to say something about using Elaine's death on my program. I thought maybe she would ask me not to do it. I was wrong. Dandy never said a word until I pulled up to let her out in front of the Chronicle building.

I didn't think she was even going to say anything then because she got out and started to close the door. But Dandy leaned back into the car with tears in her eyes again and said, "Please take good care of yourself, Park. Goodbye."

Six

It was a few minutes before three when I got back to KDG and Charlie handed me the evening's script, all typed and ready to go. Ready, that is, except for my contribution . . . the special crime report on Elaine Doherty.

My chair made its usual welcoming screech as I flopped into it. I tossed Charlie's script on the desk and sat there trying to work up enthusiasm for getting my part of it done. After a few minutes, Charlie came over and leaned a hip against my desk.

"Park, are you feeling alright?"

"Sure, I'm fine. Peachy keen, in fact."

She grimaced and shook her head at me. "That's hard to believe. You look like you just lost your best friend. Is there anything I can do?"

"No, thanks. I'm fine."

Charlie shrugged a little and went back to organizing the residue of notes and clippings left over from preparing the night's script. We store such things in files for future reference.

I shuffled some stuff around on my desk, too . . . more for appearance sake than anything else. But my efforts must not have appeared the way I intended because Charlie leaned forward after a while and said, "Park, you can tell me to mind my own business, but if you'd like to talk about whatever's on your mind, I wouldn't mind listening."

With as much of a smile as I could muster, so she'd know I appreciated her offer, I said, "Mind your own business."

"Okay. Sorry. If you change your mind, I'll be filing this stuff and keeping an eye on the wire in case something breaks before we go on the air."

As Charlie stepped out into the hall, I called to her and said, "Thanks for offering. I really do appreciate it."

She nodded and closed the door. I decided to stop feeling sorry for myself and get to work.

News writing has always come naturally to me. After picking up the grammatical nuts and bolts during my first few weeks at the L. A. Times, it's simply been a matter of sitting down and typing the words as they trickled out of my brain. Radio news isn't much different than writing for a newspaper. You just end the story a few paragraphs sooner, leaving out the minor details as required to fit the time available.

I pulled my typewriter closer, rolled in a piece of paper and sat there staring at the keys, waiting for the trickle to start. Ten minutes later I was still waiting.

The plumbing through which my scintillating prose normally flowed was stopped up. Of course, I knew very well what the problem was. It was that damn woman. Dandy was up there in my head plugging up the pipes with mental images of everything I was losing by not picking up the phone and working things out with her.

No, I wasn't going to do that. Things were best left just the way they were. So I concentrated on swapping my mental pictures of Dandy for the ones I had of Elaine Doherty out on the coast highway.

Finally the ideas jelled and the words started to flow. I typed about two minutes' worth of those words and attached them to the end of Charlie's script. It was quarter to five. I had an hour left to familiarize myself with the script and make any editing changes that occurred to me.

As I read out loud, the words fit my pace and delivery style like good song lyrics fit a melody. That was Charlie for you. She'd studied my style until she had it down perfectly.

It's not that my way of reading the news is better than anybody else's, it's just different. I try to give the words a life of their own . . . to emphasize them in a way that underscores the significance of the story. Sometimes it sounds a little corny to me, but the people of this fair city seem to like it.

At the six o'clock hour in San Francisco there are a total of five news broadcasts, four live music shows—including one featuring Wayne King's orchestra and another with Richard Himber—and a religious program. With all that to choose from, The News with Parker T. Atkins was the show more people tuned-in to than any other. So whatever we were doing, we must be doing it right.

Around five-thirty, Charlie returned to tell me that the wire was clear and she was going home. As always, Charlie reminded me that she would be listening to make sure I didn't louse up her hard work. I told her I'd do my best not to disappoint her and we said goodnight.

At quarter to six I picked up my script and wandered down the hall to the business end of KDG. The station has a couple of rooms that serve as studios, but the one I use is more like a closet than a room. It is referred to as an announcer's booth and it barely contains a small desk, a chair and a microphone. There's also a window in front of the desk that allows for nonverbal communication with the engineer in his control room. Mostly the booth is used by staff announcers for reading commercial messages and the station identifications you hear between programs.

One of those staff announcers, Dick Stewart, was occupying the booth when I arrived. He moved out of the way so I could arrange my script on the desk. Then, as the last few notes of a Jimmy Dorsey recording faded away into the ether and the engineer on the other side of our window pointed a finger at him, Dick leaned over my shoulder and spoke into the microphone.

"And that concludes our program of popular recorded music brought to you by The Emporium, located in downtown San Francisco at eight-thirty-five Market Street. Remember, for the finest in clothing, gifts and accessories, turn to The Big E . . . The Emporium.

"Be sure to tune in again tomorrow afternoon at five p.m. for another hour of the best popular music on record. Now, stay tuned for The News With Parker T. Atkins."

The engineer spun a record of some organist playing the station's adopted theme song, San Francisco. After a few seconds he faded the volume and pointed in our direction once more. Dick leaned over my shoulder again and said, "You are listening to radio station KDG at seven-hundred and forty kilocycles on the dial, serving the greater San Francisco Bay area with the finest in modern broadcast programming."

The organ music came up again for a few more seconds, faded out completely, and Dick got the engineer's finger yet again. "Ladies and gentlemen, it's six o'clock in San Francisco, time for The News With Parker T. Atkins, brought to you by the Crocker First National Bank. Now, Parker T. Atkins."

While Dick slipped out of the booth, I pointed my mouth in the general direction of the microphone and said, "Good evening San Francisco, here is your news . . . ."

I spent the next twenty-six minutes—less two minutes for commercial breaks—telling San Francisco all about the strikes, the crashed airliner, the naughty principal in Santa Cruz, and several other things, including the progress of Amelia Earhart. Finally, we got through the sports—the New York Giants took over first place in the National League by beating Pittsburgh nine to five—and there remained only the weather forecast and my special crime report. I glanced at the big clock on the wall behind the engineer. We were right on the money.

"Those of you who will be out and about tomorrow can expect another fair day with mild temperatures in the low seventies, once the morning overcast clears."

After a momentary pause, I announced, "Now, San Francisco, we bring you a KDG special crime report. This story is of particular interest to your reporter because it involves a murder I witnessed.

"It happened out on fog-shrouded Highway One south of Daly City around three a.m. Sunday morning. There was a woman out there on that lonely road . . . an attractive young woman named Elaine Doherty . . . and someone wanted her dead.

"Elaine Doherty's murderer must have pursued her for some time. We don't yet know where the pursuit began, nor where it might have ended had Miss Doherty's car not run out of gasoline.

"At the time, I was driving along the same road in the northbound direction. Suddenly, Elaine Doherty appeared out of the fog, wearing a white evening dress and running as if all the devils of the underworld were right behind her. As I turned my car around to render what assistance I could, a new black or dark colored Lincoln Zephyr sped by, heading in Miss Doherty's direction at breakneck speed.

"I pursued the Lincoln, thinking to warn the driver of Miss Doherty's presence in the roadway ahead so that he might miss her. But the driver of that Lincoln did not intend to miss Elaine Doherty. He intended to kill her.

"As I watched, the speeding Lincoln bore down on the young woman. She heard the car coming and was running across the highway to escape it when the large sedan deliberately swerved, smashing into Elaine Doherty and catapulting her mangled body to the side of the road. The Lincoln never even slowed down.

"When I found her, Elaine Doherty was dead . . . her brightly burning flame of life extinguished forever on that cold, dark, foggy road. Why was Elaine Doherty killed? We don't know. Who killed her? We don't know that, either. The answers to these questions—to the mystery of Elaine Doherty's tragic death—are out there . . . somewhere . . . and your reporter has vowed to find them. And, San Francisco, you can help in this quest for the truth.

"If you know of any facts pertaining to this murder, or if you've seen a dark-colored Lincoln Zephyr with a damaged left front fender, contact radio station KDG by calling Douglas two-two-two-four . . . Douglas two-two-two-four . . . and tell us what you know. All of the pertinent information we receive will be promptly forwarded to the proper authorities at the San Mateo County Sheriff's office to assist them in their investigation of Elaine Doherty's death.

"And that's your news for Monday, June seventh. This is Parker T. Atkins. Goodnight, San Francisco."

The engineer spun the organ recording of San Francisco again while Dick Stewart and I squeezed past each other once more. He said, "Nice job on the crime report . . . very dramatic."

The telephone on my desk was ringing when I returned to the office. I picked it up and Bea, the night switchboard operator, said, "Mister Atkins, I have a call for you from a man who says his name is Jacob Doherty. Shall I put it through?"

The part of me that was hoping Dandy might be calling was disappointed, but the rest of me was suddenly very curious. I told Bea to put him on.

The line clicked loudly in my ear and I said, "This is Parker Atkins."

"Atkins, this is Jacob Doherty calling."

His voice was hard, with a rasp that might have come from age or hard living, or both. "Yes, Mister Doherty, what can I do for you?"

"I just heard your radio broadcast. You and I need to sit down and talk some."

There was no malice or anger in Jacob Doherty's tone. He was just stating an opinion. Since it happened to be an opinion I shared, I said, "I agree, Mister Doherty. When and where?"

"Come by my office on pier forty-two at nine tonight. The big freight doors will be closed, but you can come in through the small door next to them. Somebody will be there to bring you up to my office."

I was about to say I'd be there, but the line was already dead. Apparently Jacob Doherty wasn't one for idle conversation.

Seven

The Embarcadero extends north and south from the Ferry Building at the foot of Market Street, and by day, it is the busiest street in The City. Men scurry and machines lumber up and down the waterfront, moving tons of cargo and thousands of passengers through the Port of San Francisco every day. It's a rowdy scene of perpetual motion verging on pandemonium from dawn 'til dusk.

By night, however, The Embarcadero is a wide, empty thoroughfare with no apparent purpose beyond providing a quiet haven for winos and bums. The Spanish mission facades of the warehouses that line the docks dissolve into deep shadow, becoming immense indistinguishable shapes separated only by narrow gaps through which an occasional ship's hull and spidery superstructure are dimly silhouetted against the distant lights of Oakland across the bay.

The illuminated clock in the Ferry Building's tower showed ten minutes to nine when I turned right onto The Embarcadero from Market Street. Though I'd never been to pier forty-two, I knew I was headed in the right direction because the odd-numbered piers run north of the Ferry Building and the even numbers are to the south.

The forties begin just above China Basin. By the time I reached them, my headlights and an occasional squeak from the Ford's springs as they complained about the uneven pavement were the only signs of life for miles around. The small parking area in front of pier forty-two was empty and I swung in slowly, letting my lights play over the huge red letters on the front of the building that spelled out, "Pacific Eastern Line."

On the telephone, Jacob Doherty told me to use the small entrance next to the large freight doors. With no other cars around and no lights visible either outside or inside the building, I wondered if I might find that door locked—if Jacob Doherty had changed his mind about meeting me.

The metal doorknob was already cold and damp with dew, but it turned freely. I let the door swing open on hinges that shared a common ancestry with my office chair. They squealed loudly, announcing my arrival to whoever was waiting for me inside. A single light bulb glowed feebly somewhere in the depths of the warehouse, casting dim shadows of crates, barrels and odd shapes under tarps.

There was a lot more to smell than there was to see. The dank air inside was permeated with a raucous mixture of spices, tea leaves and other exotic substances I couldn't begin to identify.

I stood there in the doorway a while, waiting for someone to welcome me. When nothing happened, I stepped inside and said loudly, "Hello? Anybody here?"

"Close the door and walk toward the light."

It was not a greeting that made me feel particularly welcome. The booming basso voce' that echoed off the warehouse rafters had an edge about it that left me fighting a temptation to turn around and get the hell out of there while I still could. But the voice also had a folksy sort of seaman's twang that almost forgave its brusqueness.

I closed the door and moved forward cautiously through the gloom. The shape of a large man appeared between me and the light. There was a knit watch cap on his head and the glint of a large knife grip protruding from a scabbard on his left hip. As I approached, the rest of his costume took form—baggy denim pants and a heavy wool shirt that looked much too warm for our mild June climate.

"Stop there."

I stopped.

"Put your arms out and lean against that there crate."

He was gesturing toward a large wooden shipping crate on my left. I did as I was told without protest.

He stepped closer and said, "Spread your feet apart."

When I had complied with that command, he proceeded to pat me down with a thoroughness that any cop in the land would have admired. I wondered where he might have picked up that particular talent.

"Alright, ya can turn around now."

I turned around and looked into a face that didn't go with the man's nautical costume. It was well scrubbed and clean shaven with neatly trimmed sideburns. It was also a face I'd seen earlier in the day. It took me a moment, but when I imagined him in a white shirt, black tie and vest, I recognized the houseman who'd admitted Dandy and me to the Dohertys' mansion.

"Captain Doherty is waitin' for ya in his office. The stairs is over there. Go up 'em nice and gentle. I'll be right behind ya."

Climbing the wooden steps, I wondered if all Jacob Doherty's visitors were welcomed in this manner or if I was being accorded special treatment. The latter seemed more likely, but I couldn't imagine why Doherty thought such precautions were necessary. Maybe he didn't. Maybe this was just a little friendly intimidation to impress me with Doherty's power. I wasn't impressed.

At the top of the stairs, the houseman pointed down a rough wooden-floored hallway with doors on both sides. About halfway down the hall, he put a hand on my shoulder to stop me and rapped his knuckles on the nearest door. In a voice that was muffled by the door, but still recognizable from our telephone conversation, Jacob Doherty told us to come in.

His thin, deeply-lined face was topped off by a tangled mop of shock white hair and large, bushy eyebrows of the same color. Below the eyebrows were two cold gray eyes that watched intently and missed nothing. Jacob Doherty's hands, resting on the desk in front of him, were large and gnarled with arthritis.

"Sit down there, Atkins."

As I moved toward the high-backed chair he'd indicated, Doherty addressed his houseman. "Alec, this fellow and I have matters to discuss. Wait outside."

The bass voice said, "Aye, Captain." A moment later, I heard the office door close.

Jacob Doherty and I stared at each other for several seconds. His aforementioned cold gray eyes were doing their best to intimidate, but as a cop I'd learned how to handle a stare-down. At one time I'd been quite good at it. I still was. Doherty finally frowned and glanced away long enough to pick up a vicious-looking dagger-like letter opener.

He leaned back, slapped the letter opener across his palm, and said, "You seem to think you can exploit my granddaughter's death to benefit your radio station. I don't much like that."

"And I don't much like hearing you say that, Mister Doherty. I also don't much like watching young women get killed. I might not be so interested in Elaine's death if I hadn't been there to see it, but I was, and it makes me angry."

"So you take out your anger on me by harassing my other granddaughter and dragging my name through the mud on your radio broadcast. Is that how you do things, Atkins?"

"There was no mud associated with your name on my broadcast. And if Gladys had told me the truth this afternoon, there would have been no reason to harass her."

"What makes you so sure Gladys was lying?"

"I assume Gladys told you about our conversation, or maybe Alec listened at the door and gave you a report. Maybe both. Would you have believed any of that malarkey she was handing me?"

Doherty tossed his letter opener on the desk and slowly shook his head. "No, I guess I wouldn't. But Gladys was under no obligation to tell you anything in the first place, so your treatment of her was uncalled for."

"Mister Doherty, I don't enjoy badgering young women, and it's possible that I pushed Gladys too far, but I intend to find out who killed your granddaughter and why. I should think you would share that interest."

"Oh, I do. But I also pay a very great deal in taxes to support government agencies which, among other things, investigate murders. Is there any reason why I should expect you to do a better job of that than the San Mateo Sheriff?"

"No, I . . . ."

"No, you're damn right there isn't. When I found out about your visit to the house this afternoon, I made some calls and checked into your background. You aren't very reliable at all, are you? In fact, you're a drunk. Isn't that right?"

"I won't deny that I was a drunk, nor will I sit here and tell you I won't be again. But for the moment, I am very sober. And if your sources are worth a damn, they also told you that I was once a very good homicide cop in a city with enough crime to make even San Francisco look tame by comparison."

Doherty and I stared at each other again for a few seconds before he said, "Yes, I did hear that. Your former Captain in Los Angeles said something about you having a sixth sense when it came to investigating murders. In fact, he seemed to miss having you around."

When I didn't respond, the old man sighed and leaned forward on his desk. "Atkins, the truth is I think I like you. More to the point, I need you."

There wasn't much Doherty could have said that would have surprised me more. If he was looking for a reaction, he got it. "You need me? Would you mind explaining that?"

"As you can plainly see, I'm an old man. There was a time . . . ." He paused and shook his head. "No, you don't need to hear all that. It's enough to say that I don't get around as well as I used to. And I can't rely on my son in matters like this because . . . well, as much as it pains me to say it, Rutherford is worthless outside of a business office. Maybe if I'd been around more when the boy was growing up . . . ."

"I'm not following you, Mister Doherty. What is it that you need me for that you or your son can't do?"

His eyebrows went up in what looked to me like a genuine expression of surprise. "Why, exactly what you're doing . . . finding my granddaughter's murderer."

"What happened to all that faith you had in government agencies?"

"Alright, I guess I've got that coming. I'm . . . I'm sorry for being so hard on you before. I just needed to be sure you were really the man I thought you were."

I was watching his expression closely. It was clear that apologies didn't come easy to Jacob Doherty. If he was willing to make one, it meant Doherty wanted something from me in the worst way. He confirmed that fact by pulling an inch-thick bundle of cash out of his drawer and tossing it across the desk. The top bill had Benjamin Franklin's picture on it.

"Atkins, that's five thousand dollars there. It's yours. And you get another five when you tell me who killed Elaine."

Doherty's pile of bills sat there on his desk commanding my attention. It isn't everyday that you get to see an amount nearly equal to your annual income all in one tidy little stack. I looked at it, thought about what I could do with it, and asked the obvious question.

"Mister Doherty, just exactly what is it you expect to buy with that?"

It didn't appear to be the response he was looking for. "I told you. I want you to find out who killed my granddaughter."

"You can have that for nothing, so you must expect something else."

Doherty clasped his big hands on the desk in a gesture of sincerity and said, "Only that you conduct your investigation independently and discreetly."

"Meaning that you don't want me to tell the cops what I find out and I can't use the story on my news broadcasts. Is that it?"

"Essentially, yes."

"I can think of only one reason for you to make such a generous offer. There must be something about all this you don't want to become a matter of public record. And when I find Elaine's murderer, there's only one way to avoid a public trial and all the publicity that would go along with it. That would be if the killer were to quietly disappear before the police found him."

"Very good, Atkins. You catch on quickly. Of course, I wouldn't expect you to take care of the last detail. I'm quite capable of arranging that on my own."

It took just about all the willpower I had in me, but I pushed the money back across the desk and said, "I'm sorry, Mister Doherty, but I already have an employer."

A shrewd smile crossed his thin lips. "Would you feel the same if I doubled my offer?"

Having made it over the first tempting hurdle, it was easier to get past the second, but not much. It helped a little that I considered his offer an insult to what was left of my integrity.

I concentrated on that thought and said, "I'm obviously not the man you thought I was, after all. There is no amount of money that will make me help you hide your family secrets by committing another murder."

Abruptly, Doherty grabbed the five grand and dropped it back into his desk drawer. "Then our conversation is over." His eyes narrowed and turned even colder. "You are going to regret the choice you just made. When you change your mind, come and see me. My offer may still be on the table." In a louder voice, he said, "Alec, come in here!"

Not knowing what to expect, I stood quickly as Alec burst through the office door. He glared at me and crouched slightly. His hand was already hovering over the knife on his hip when Doherty said, "Alec, Atkins and I are through talking. Take him back to his car."

The big man relaxed a little, but his hand remained at his hip as he held the door open for me. Two minutes later I was back on The Embarcadero, headed north.

Eight

The Fillmore is a workingman's neighborhood where folks go to bed early on weeknights. So when I got home about eleven, the streets were nearly as deserted as the waterfront.

I usually park across from my apartment, but the spaces there were all taken by that hour so I continued east on McAllister and found a spot at the end of the block, near Fillmore Street. From there I jay-walked across McAllister and headed back up the block toward the Alta Apartments.

Fog was descending upon The City as I walked up the empty sidewalk, its fine silvery mist illuminated by the streetlights as the tiny droplets drifted silently to the ground. I listened to my footsteps on the damp concrete and thought about Jacob Doherty's offer. He'd been willing to part with ten—maybe even twenty—grand just to get his hands on Elaine's murderer before the cops did. And from the sound of it, Doherty was fully prepared to commit his own murder just to protect some dark family secret.

Picturing the killer behind the wheel of his Lincoln, I wondered if he had any idea how badly Doherty wanted him dead. Or why. Just then my mental picture of the Lincoln triggered another, more recent, memory. One of the cars along the curb where I usually park was a big black sedan. Not a Lincoln, but a new Buick. Expensive cars like that don't belong in a working-class neighborhood. What the hell was it doing here?

I was less than fifty feet from the steps up to the entrance of the Alta Apartments. The curb directly in front of those steps is a red zone, so I stepped behind the last car on my side of the street before the empty section of curb and looked across McAllister.

Sure enough, directly opposite the entrance to my apartment building was a shiny new Buick sedan with enough chromium plating adorning its long hood and bulging fenders to gussy up an entire fleet of lesser automobiles. And because it was parked within a few yards of a streetlight, I could see another feature about the car that interested me. There was someone inside—a big man—sitting next to the open driver's window.

While I was standing there looking at him, he turned to look at me. It was dark out there on Highway One and he'd only been in my headlights for an instant, but as our eyes met now, I knew who the man in the Buick was and why he was there. And he knew I knew.

The killer moved quickly to open the car door, and in the same instant, I made my decision. Turning back toward Fillmore Street, I ran like hell. The Buick's starter whined, followed immediately by the healthy rumble of an eight cylinder engine. I was glad he decided to come after me in the car, instead of on foot. It was going to take him some time to jockey the big sedan out of that parking space.

As I came to the corner, there was a loud bang and the sound of metal scraping metal. He'd gotten impatient. This guy was hard as hell on fenders.

I swung left and ran down the sidewalk along Fillmore for about thirty yards until I came to the recessed doorway of an office building. I ducked in just before screeching tires said the Buick was rounding the corner behind me.

He'd seen me turn onto Fillmore, but when he got there I was out of sight. Now he was creeping along, searching both sides of the street for me. I knew he'd see me in the doorway. In fact, I was counting on it.

The only way a man on foot can outrun someone in a car is by going where the car can't go. My plan was to wait until he came by, then jump out of the doorway and run back the way I'd come, forcing him to either drive around the block or try to make a u-turn between the cars parked on both sides of the street. Either way, I'd have time to put some distance between the Buick and me.

I watched the twin beams of his headlights moving slowly up the street past my doorway. A moment later the huge radiator grille at the front of the Buick's long hood slid into view. Just another second or two.

When I judged that about half of the hood had passed, I bolted out of the doorway. As I turned right, I saw him raise a big revolver in his left hand. In that narrow canyon between the buildings along Fillmore, his shot sounded like a howitzer.

He knew something about leading a moving target. His bullet smacked into the building to my right about a foot in front of me and chest high. The slug ricocheted away and sandstone chips exploded from the wall, peppering my face like buckshot.

I was still twenty yards from the corner when his tires squealed again and the Buick's transmission started whining at a high pitch. Hell! He was backing up!

I cursed myself for not considering the fact that cars do go backwards as well as forward. Suddenly he was abreast of me. I chanced falling on my face to take a look. He was busy trying to line up another shot and keep the Buick backing straight at the same time, but I was staring straight down the barrel of his revolver.

I dived for the sidewalk behind the last parked car on the block as he fired his second shot. I hit the concrete hard; a slug pinged off metal somewhere over my head and I heard him stomp on the brakes again.

The next sound came from the building behind me. Some guy a few floors up yelled out his window, "Hey! What the hell's going on down there? Stop shooting off that damned gun!"

I looked around and realized half the windows on the block were lighting up. Suddenly there was an entire neighborhood full of witnesses watching the guy try to blow my brains out. He must have noticed the same thing. His tires squealed one last time as he shifted out of reverse and scooted off down Fillmore. I got to my knees just in time to see the Buick's taillights disappear around the corner onto Golden Gate.

Teetering on rubber legs, I stood up and dusted myself off. My savior on the third floor yelled down, "Hey, mister, are you okay?"

I waved at him and sauntered shakily around the corner onto McAllister. Sirens were wailing a few blocks away when I finally got my key to work and disappeared through the Alta Apartments' front door.

Fortunately, my apartment is only one floor up. The only way I could have climbed another flight would have been on my hands and knees. I threw the dead bolt and flopped onto the couch. God, I wanted a drink!

Instead, I sat there in the dark waiting for the effects of a massive adrenalin overdose to wear off. When it felt like my legs might be up to the job, I went down the hall to the bathroom and turned on the light.

The guy in the mirror looked like he'd taken a face full of bird shot. I was covered with streaks of blood from cuts caused by the sandstone splinters that hit me when the killer's first shot ricocheted off the building. I washed the blood away and things looked a little better. There were only a few real cuts and they weren't deep. After I covered the damage with gauze and adhesive tape, I took a look at the rest of me.

My shirt had splatters of blood on it and both knees of my slacks were torn from their encounter with Fillmore Street's sidewalk. I changed into fresh clothes and stuffed just about everything else from my closet and dresser into an old leather suitcase. In the kitchen I reached up and felt around on the top shelf of the cabinet next to the sink until I found the heavy little cardboard box and the chamois sack hidden there.

Sitting at the table, I pulled my old Colt Detective Special out of the sack. With fingers that were none too steady, I flipped the chamber open and loaded five rounds from the cardboard box of thirty-eight caliber ammunition. The little revolver went into my right coat pocket and five more rounds went into my left pocket. The ammo box slipped neatly between some shirts in my suitcase.

I took one last look around the apartment to be sure I hadn't forgotten to turn something off. Finally, I locked the door and headed for my trusty Ford.

There was still a police cruiser double-parked around the corner on Fillmore, but the cops who belonged to it were nowhere to be seen. I felt a little guilty about leaving them to sort things out for themselves, but it had already been a long damned day and I wasn't in the mood to go downtown and spend the rest of it answering questions.

I drove down Mission, past San Jose Avenue, and pulled into the Mission Auto Court. I knew the place because I'd found their advertisement in the Auto Club guide book and spent my first couple of weeks in San Francisco there. The night clerk even remembered me. We were old chums.

At one-fifteen, I finally climbed into my rented bed. I'd kept an eye on the rear view mirror all the way from my apartment and was reasonably certain no one followed me, so I figured I was safe for the moment. I also figured I was damned lucky to have survived my own stupidity.

What I'd said in my broadcast about witnessing the murder of Elaine Doherty was just asking for trouble. My journalistic sense had clearly gotten in the way of my common sense.

Now I would have to be on guard every minute until Elaine's killer and whoever else was involved in this thing were behind bars. It wasn't a very pleasant way to live, but I'd done it before. I could do it again.

As I drifted off, Dandy came strolling into my dreams. At first she was terribly concerned and making a big fuss about the cuts on my face. Then she was running down Highway One in the fog and a big black sedan with vicious chrome teeth for a grille was nipping at her heels.

Nine

8:00 a.m.—Tuesday—June 8, 1937

Tuesday morning I drove in to work with the commuters from Daly City and points south. We crept two abreast along Mission Boulevard in a bumper-to-bumper stream of impatient humanity.

I bid my fellow travelers adieu at Third Street, where I turned left and cut across to Market. Being later than usual, finding a parking place require a couple of circuits around the block. I took advantage of the opportunity to canvas the area for big black sedans. I saw none that gave me cause for alarm.

With a little luck I got through KDG's lobby and down the hall to our office without anyone inquiring about the wads of gauze stuck to my face. Charlie wasn't there when I came in, but the stacks of morning papers on her desk told me she wasn't far away.

Changing the normal routine slightly, I draped my coat over the back of my chair instead of hanging it on the coat tree. Carrying a gun to protect yourself from bad guys didn't make much sense unless you kept it handy.

My chair was happy to see me. It greeted me with a cacophonous chorus of squeals as I sat down to look at the pile of telephone message slips from Monday night. There were an even dozen of them, all responses to my broadcast plea for help in finding Elaine Doherty's killer.

Bea's neatly printed notations helped me make short work of separating the wheat from the chaff. Eleven of the messages went directly into the round file on the floor next to my desk because they either offered information that clearly had nothing to do with the price of cheese in Denmark or they were marked with the word "loony"—Bea's code for a caller who isn't cooking on all four burners.

The remaining message, however, interested me. It was from one Osgood Bledsoe who identified himself as the General Manager of the Howard Automobile Company. In Bea's shorthand, Bledsoe's message read, "Has info re new Linc traded by cstmr."

A check of the phone directory raised my level of interest in Osgood Bledsoe several more notches. The Howard Automobile Company was San Francisco's authorized Buick dealer. I jotted their address down on the message and slipped it into my shirt pocket. While I was doing that, Charlie walked in.

She wished me a good morning, stopped, cocked her head a little to one side, and said, "Park, you really ought to wait until you've had some coffee before you shave in the morning."

I made a face at her. "You're a regular Charlie McCarthy, aren't ya?"

Tossing several feet of yellow wire service copy on her desk, she sat down facing me. "Well? Are you going to explain or just sit there and tell me everything's peachy keen again?"

Since Charlie already knew most of what had happened up until the previous night, and because it seemed like a good idea for someone besides me to know all the details, I told her the whole story, beginning with Doherty's call after the broadcast and ending with my narrow escape on Fillmore Street. Charlie listened attentively throughout the entire sordid tale.

When I was done, she took a deep breath and said, "Whew! You had quite a night."

"That's one way to put it."

"What are the police doing about all this?"

"I don't know. I didn't talk to them."

"Why in heaven's name not?"

"Like you said, it was quite a night. I wasn't in the mood to answer a bunch of questions."

"But they don't know who they're looking for."

"Neither do I. I'm sure my neighbors told the cops what happened just as well as I could . . . maybe someone even got the Buick's license number. I sure didn't."

"So what are you going to do now?"

"I'm gonna find the guy."

"How?"

"I've got a few things to go on." I described the Rose Bowl ticket stub I found in Gladys' Oldsmobile and the call from Osgood Bledsoe.

"Well, the Buick dealer might be a good lead, but I doubt if the Rose Bowl angle will get you far. Have you ever been there?"

"Never had the pleasure."

"I have. The place is huge. They say the dance floor alone is half an acre. On a good night they jam three thousand people in that place. It's pretty unlikely anyone will remember if Elaine Doherty was there or not."

It surprised me that Charlie knew so much about a dance pavilion. Maybe I'd underestimated the extent of her social life. I was tempted to ask about it.

Instead I said, "Probably not, but you never know. I have to follow up on every reasonable lead." I nodded toward the newspapers and wire service copy on her desk. "What's going on this morning?"

Charlie picked up her legal pad and started summarizing the day's headline stories. She was telling me about an Assistant Sergeant at Arms in the State Legislature who'd been indicted for bribery when the office door suddenly flew open and smashed into the wall behind it with a crash. The little Colt was already out of my coat pocket by the time I realized it was Kastner who'd burst into our office.

Kastner jabbed a pudgy finger at me and yelled, "Mister, I want to talk to you." He turned to Charlie and in a slightly calmer tone said, "Excuse us, Miss."

Charlie left in a hurry and Kastner marched up to my desk. His face was so flushed it matched his maroon bow tie which made him look like someone had tied one of his chins in a knot.

"Atkins, would you care to hazard a guess as to who got me out of bed with a telephone call at ten-fifteen last night?"

Judging from his mood, it didn't seem likely that Mayor Rossi had called with another compliment on my program. I shook my head.

"Well, I'll tell you. It was Jacob Doherty, only one of the richest, most influential men in this city."

Of course, the minute he said Doherty's name I remembered the old man's warning that I would regret my decision not to accept his offer. Apparently he was using Kastner to show me the error of my ways.

"And do you have any idea why he called me? You should. Doherty said he'd already discussed it with you."

"Let me guess. Doherty told you he didn't like my story on his daughter's death."

"That's not exactly the way he put it, but you've got the general idea. Specifically, Jacob Doherty said you libeled him and if it happens again he's going to sue the pants off me and this radio station."

"Did you listen to the program, Mister Kastner?"

He looked a little uncomfortable. "Why, no. I was . . . ."

I pulled Monday night's script out of the filing cabinet behind me and shoved the sheaf of papers into his hand. "There's last night's script, exactly as broadcast. The Doherty story is on the last couple of pages. Read it. If you find any hint of libel in there, I'll hand you my resignation here and now."

Kastner stared at the script in his hand for a moment as if deciding what to do. Finally, he tossed it on my desk and said, "Alright, Parker. I'll take your word for that. Maybe he was bluffing. But that doesn't matter. Whatever the reason, the man is mad as hell. We can't go around upsetting people like Jacob Doherty that way."

"Mister Kastner, when you hired me you said you wanted a first class news program with some bite to it. You told me to go all out on attacking crime in San Francisco. Isn't that right?"

"Yes, but . . . ."

"Okay, that's exactly what I was doing last night—attacking the person or persons who committed a brutal, cold-blooded murder."

He frowned. "Who's murder? What are you talking about?"

I stifled an urge to tell him he ought to listen to his own radio station, or at least read a newspaper once in a while and said, "Elaine Doherty's murder."

"Elaine Doherty? Who's she?"

"Jacob Doherty's granddaughter and she was murdered—deliberately run down by an automobile out on the coast highway Saturday night. I saw it happen."

"You saw it? And that's what you reported on your broadcast?"

"Exactly. And just to make things even more interesting, the man who killed her also took a couple of shots at me last night."

He had picked up the script and was thumbing through it when I said that. Kastner's head jerked up and he looked at me as if noticing my bandages for the first time, although they were pretty darn hard to miss.

"Is that what happened to your face?"

"More or less."

Kastner slumped into Charlie's chair with the script still in his hands. "Well, if all you did was report on a murder you witnessed, what the hell is Doherty so upset about?"

I wasn't about to tell Kastner the details of my meeting with Jacob Doherty. He probably wouldn't have believed me anyway. Instead, I gave him something close.

"I'm not sure about this, but I think Doherty is trying to keep something under wraps and the more attention Elaine's death attracts, the more likely someone will stumble onto his secret."

Kastner's face changed colors again. This time he went pale as parchment. "You don't think Doherty killed his own granddaughter, do you?"

"No, nothing like that."

He sighed audibly, relieved that I wasn't going to call one of the richest men in town a murderer on my next broadcast. After a moment of thought, Kastner said, "Parker, I'm in a ticklish spot here. I don't want to tell you how to do your job, but Jacob Doherty is in a position to do us a lot of damage if he wants to."

My chair let out an unusually loud shriek as I leaned back. "I understand that, Mister Kastner, but we may have the crime story of the year here. And Doherty sure as hell won't risk even more publicity by suing us. I think we've got to see this through."

"Have any of the papers or the other stations picked this up yet?"

"No, they're reporting Miss Doherty's death as an accident. So far, we have an exclusive."

He looked as if he wasn't sure whether that was good or not and said, "What about the police? What do they say about all of this?"

"It happened in the San Mateo County Sheriff's jurisdiction. I've been working with the deputy who got the case. At the very least, they're calling it a hit-and-run."

"And you're absolutely certain of your facts?"

"Absolutely."

He sighed again like he was about to say something he was going to regret. "Alright, Parker, stay on it. But go as easy on the Doherty family as you can, will you? And be careful. I don't need you gettin' yourself killed over this thing."

"I'll do my best on both scores."

Kastner stood up, dropped the script back on my desk, and walked to the door. Opening it, he turned and said, "And, for chrissake, get your damned chair fixed. That squeaking drives me crazy."

I nodded and Kastner walked out the door. No more than thirty seconds later, Charlie came back. "What in heaven's name was that all about? Do we still have jobs?"

I smiled. "Barely, but yes."

"He looked like he was going to explode!"

"It seems Jacob Doherty called him last night after I left and tried to light a fire under my tail by threatening to sue Kastner if we continued our series on Elaine's murder."

"So we drop the story, right?"

"Wrong. Kastner says stay on it."

"You're joking!"

"Nope. And I have to give the man credit. Kastner is showing some courage I would have bet he didn't have."

"I think you deserve the credit. How did you ever talk him out of killing the story?"

"Let's save that for another time. We've got some work to do."

"You want me to finish going through this stuff?" She held up her legal pad.

"No, I've got a hell of a lot to do and very little time to do it. Use your judgment on the stories for tonight and leave me about three minutes. I'll be back as soon as I can this afternoon."

Charlie stopped me on my way out. "Park, I saw what you got out of your coat pocket when Kastner came barging in here. This thing is starting to scare me. Be careful, will you?"

I smiled back at her. "Count on it, sweetheart."

Fifteen minutes later I was riding the Chronicle's elevator down to their basement. The Chron's morgue is a gloomy gymnasium-sized room crowded with filing cabinets and shelves full of old newspapers that date clear back to before Hector was a pup. There are also a few worktables and a couple of desks. Bobby Newmann was sitting at one of those desks when I stepped out of the elevator.

Newmann is a big gruff-lookin' guy with a lot of character in his face. He reminds me of Harry Carey with a receding hair line. He looked up and frowned at me.

"Atkins, I ain't talkin' to you."

I sat on a corner of his desk and said, "Welcome to the club. What, specifically, is your complaint about the behavior of Parker T. Atkins?"

"Hell, I got a whole list of complaints about you, buddy. Hey, what in tarnation happened to your face?"

"I shaved before my first cup of coffee this morning. What's on your list?"

Newmann glowered at the humor I'd borrowed from Charlie and said, "Well, number one, I asked you yesterday if you had somethin' cookin' with the Doherty gal's death and you said no. Then I listen to your broadcast last night and find out you told me a great big fib."

"Not exactly true, Bobby," I lied. "I wasn't sure there was really anything to it until after I talked to you. You'd be even madder if I'd told you about it and the whole thing turned out to be a bunch of hot air, wouldn't you?"

Bobby glared at me. "Alright, I know you're lyin' again, but your story sounds good. I'll let you off the hook on that one."

"Next complaint?"

"I ask a simple little favor in exchange for helpin' you out and what happens? You waltz in here empty-handed! My mouth's been waterin' for those macaroon tarts all morning. Where the hell are they?"

"That's kind of a long story, Bobby."

He folded his arms across his considerable chest. "I'm all ears."

"Well, it's this way. I'd planned to stop at Schubert's this morning on my way in and pick up the tarts nice and fresh, but there was a little trouble last night and I ended up staying at an auto court on the other side of town."

Bobby looked at my face and said, "That trouble have anything to do with the mummy makeup you're wearin'?"

I nodded. "Any other complaints on your list?"

"Yeah, but you've probably already got excuses made up for them, too." He opened his top drawer and pulled out a handful of clippings. "Here's all I got on the Dohertys."

I started through them. "Anything interesting?"

"Not a blessed thing. All society stories and community service awards . . . stuff like that."

"Any pictures of Elaine Doherty in here?"

"Yeah, there's a pretty decent one on the bottom."

I flipped through to the last clipping and, sure enough, there was a two-column photo of a smiling Elaine Doherty. The article also had Dandy Harrison's byline.

"Can I borrow this one, Bobby?"

"You can keep 'em all. They're extras."

"Thanks. And I'll get you those tarts from Schubert's just as soon as things calm down. I promise."

Bobby looked me in the eye. "Sure. And watch yourself, buddy. I don't want anything happenin' to you before you keep that promise."

In the elevator again, I punched the third floor button. I hadn't planned on going up to Dandy's office, but seeing her byline and being this close to her . . . well, at least I could make sure she was alright.

The society staff rated. Their brightly-lit, cheery offices made Bobby's place look like a dungeon. I poked my head in Dandy's cubicle and my heart sank a little. Her chair was empty.

Susie-somebody, a little red-headed secretary with bright green eyes I remembered from previous visits to Dandy's domain, recognized me and came over. "Good morning, Mister Atkins. Miss Harrison isn't here today. She called in earlier and said she was going to do some interviews and wouldn't be back until tomorrow."

I nodded glumly. "What about her column? Is somebody else writing it?"

"Oh, no. She sent it over by messenger a little while ago."

"Okay," I sighed. "Thanks, Susie."

"You're welcome, Mister Atkins."

As I turned to leave, Susie tugged at my coat sleeve and stepped closer so she wouldn't be overheard. "It's none of my business, Mister Atkins, but Dandy was real upset yesterday afternoon. And, well . . . Dandy is ever so sweet. I just hate to see her all torn up like that."

I gave her a cheer-up smile. "I don't like it either, Susie. I'm going to see what I can do to make things better."

Susie beamed at me as if I'd just made all the problems of the world go away. "That's real good, Mister Atkins. You're sweet, too. You take care of yourself now."

Riding back down the elevator, it occurred to me that an awful lot of people were suddenly concerned about my welfare and telling me to take care of myself. First Kastner told me to be careful, then Charlie and Bobby Newmann. Now Susie wanted me to take care of myself. Hell, maybe I just look helpless.

Ten

It was just past eleven when I walked into the Howard Automobile Company's showroom on Van Ness at O'Farrell. A salesman was at my side before I got both feet through the door, and he was well into his spiel about all the amazing new features found on the nineteen-thirty-seven Buicks before I got enough words in edgewise to explain that I was there to see Osgood Bledsoe. His disappointment was obvious, but he shrugged and led me to the General Manager's office.

Bledsoe was out when we got there, so the salesman told me to have a seat while he found the boss. I leafed through a pamphlet which reminded me on nearly every page that when better cars are built, Buick will build them.

The pamphlet also went to great lengths describing four luxurious Buick models—the Century, the Roadmaster, the Limited, and the Special. Bold text informed the reader that all four models had been thoroughly redesigned for nineteen-thirty-seven, which made this reader wonder what was so wrong with the thirty-six models that necessitated all that redesigning.

I was busy learning more about Buick engine displacements, wheel bases, and interior appointments than I could ever imagine needing to know when Osgood Bledsoe walked in. He was medium-tall and a little chunky, with slicked-back black hair. He was also enthusiastic about everything.

"Mister Atkins, it's a real pleasure to meet you. I listen to your broadcast every night, but I never expected to meet you in person. My whole family enjoys listening to you."

Like everyone else who said things like that, he meant well. But I always wonder why anyone would describe listening to my reports of strikes, murders and disasters as an enjoyable experience. I smiled my best radio celebrity smile and said, "Thank you, Mister Bledsoe. I . . . ."

"Call me Ozzie. Can I get you a cup of coffee? How about a doughnut?"

"Ah, no thanks, Ozzie. I'm here about your phone call to the station last night."

"Oh, yes. Funny thing about that. You could have knocked me over with a feather when I heard you were looking for a new Lincoln Zephyr with a banged up left front fender. I was telling the missus about it right before your broadcast. Then there you were, asking if anyone had seen the car."

"You think you've seen it?"

"I believe I have. What happened is, this fellow comes into the showroom yesterday and says he's interested in buying a sedan. Ernie—he's one of our salesmen—gives him the pitch and the guy picks out a black Limited. Only problem is, he's got a car to trade.

"So Ernie goes out to look at the fellow's car, and it's this new Zephyr. There's only a few hundred miles on the odometer and it's in perfect shape except for a bashed-in left front fender and headlight.

"Ernie asks him why he wants to get rid of a brand new Lincoln and the guy says it's his boss's car and his boss is real upset because of the fender. Says he never wants to see the damned thing again and tells this guy to go trade it in on a Buick. The fellow has the ownership registration and a blank check with him, all ready to go.

"Well, to make a long story short, Ernie comes in here and wants to know what we can give this guy in trade for his car on the Limited. Problem was, they paid something like fourteen hundred for the Zephyr and the Limited is only around twelve-fifty, so we can't give 'em half what the Lincoln's worth or we lose money on the deal.

"So Ernie goes back out to offer the guy six, figuring the sale's already out the window. A minute later, here comes Ernie back to tell me the fellow took the deal without even blinking an eye!

"Mister Atkins, I've been in the automobile business for more than ten years and I've learned to be cautious when a deal like that comes along. We checked and double-checked all the paperwork, but everything was on the level. So the guy drove out of here in the Limited and the Lincoln's back in the shop waiting for our auto body man to fix the fender."

Finding the murder vehicle this easily was too good to be true, so I had my doubts when I asked, "Can you show it to me?"

"Sure! That's why I called you in the first place."

The Lincoln was parked in a service bay at one end of the shop. As I knelt to examine the left front fender, Bledsoe said, "This is exactly the way it was when the fellow brought it in. Nothing's been touched yet."

Of course, it would take a forensic investigation to determine if there were any cloth fibers or blood stains on the fender that would tie the big sedan to Elaine Doherty, but the car matched my mental picture from Saturday night perfectly and the damage looked about right.

I climbed in and searched the seats and floorboards. Then I checked the trunk—all without finding so much as a speck of lint. The Lincoln was clean as a whistle.

"Mister Bledsoe . . . Ozzie . . . I can't say for sure, but it looks like you've found the car that killed Elaine Doherty. Do you have the name and address of the previous owner?"

Bledsoe beamed. "The contract-of-sale is in my desk. I pulled it from the master file first thing this morning because I knew you'd want to see it."

He turned to go back to his office, but I stopped him. "One more thing, Ozzie. It would be a good idea to tell your mechanics not to touch this car quite yet. The police will want their criminal investigation people to go over it for evidence."

"Say, you're right! I'll take care of that this minute."

Bledsoe had a brief discussion with his shop foreman, and we went back to his office where I copied the pertinent facts from the contract-of-sale. The previous owner of the Lincoln was not an individual, but a company called North Bay Therapeutic Enterprises. And their address wasn't a street number, but a post office box in San Rafael.

A name and street address would have been better, but that isn't how homicide investigations go. At least we had the Lincoln and a connection to the person or persons responsible for Elaine Doherty's murder.

"Ozzie, did you see the fellow who brought the Lincoln in?"

"I sure did. He sat right there in that chair while we filled out the papers."

"What did he look like?"

Bledsoe thought about it for a moment and said, "He was a big fellow . . . at least six feet . . . real broad shoulders . . . big hands."

"What about the color of his eyes and hair?"

"I think his eyes were brown, but I'm not sure. I didn't notice his hair because he was wearing a hat the whole time. I do remember that he had a sort of large square jaw."

"You said he was wearing a hat. How was he dressed otherwise?"

"Well, he was wearing a moderately expensive dark blue, double-breasted business suit. The hat was a gray fedora. I think his tie was a solid color, either dark blue or black. His shoes were good quality wing-tips, black."

Even though I didn't get close enough to judge the quality of the guy's shoes or notice the color of his tie, the description fit the man who'd shot at me the night before and driven the Lincoln Saturday night reasonably well. I complimented Bledsoe on his powers of observation.

"Oh, in the quality automobile business you learn how to spot the people who can afford what you're selling. It helps save a lot of wasted time and effort."

I wondered if Bledsoe had me figured for someone who could afford a Buick. Probably not. I asked him if there was a private telephone around I could use to make a couple of calls. He said he needed to see one of his salesmen anyway, and I was welcome to use the phone on his desk while he was gone.

While I hunted through my notebook for Will Framm's number, I dialed the station. Charlie had some telephone messages for me.

"Park, that deputy from San Mateo has called three times."

"Did he say what he wanted?"

"Yes, to talk to you. He was real clear about that. Last time he said if you didn't call him back within an hour, he was going to get a warrant and have you arrested!"

I could only think of two or three reasons why Framm would be angry with me. The most likely was that Jacob Doherty was still trying to stir things up. Whether it was that or something else didn't really matter. I was pretty certain that if I called him, Framm would tell me to back off and leave the investigating to him. Since I didn't especially want to hear that, I got Charlie to do my dirty work.

"Charlie, call Framm for me and tell him I found the Lincoln that killed Elaine Doherty. Tell him to see Osgood Bledsoe at the Howard Automobile Company on Van Ness."

"You really found it? Aren't you going to call Framm?"

"Yes, I found it, and no, I'm not. Tell Framm . . . ."

"Park, you have to call him! He's going to have you arrested!"

"Oh, I don't think he'll go to all that trouble. Tell him the car was registered to North Bay Therapeutic Enterprises and the only address they gave was Post Office Box one-one-nine in San Rafael. Got that?"

"I got it. But, I really think . . . ."

"Thanks, Charlie. See you in a couple of hours."

I thought about talking to Ernie, the salesman who'd handled the Lincoln deal, but decided to leave that detail to Framm. It was almost twelve-fifteen and I had a fair piece of ground to cover before I could head back to the station and write my script for the evening's broadcast.

Osgood Bledsoe met me on my way out. I thanked him for his help and told him to expect someone from the San Mateo County Sheriff's office to show up before long.

"I'll watch for them personally, Mister Atkins. Say, ah . . . are you going to mention this on your broadcast tonight? I mean, are you going to say that I helped you find the car?"

"Ozzie, you can be sure I'll give credit where credit is due, but it might be safer to leave your name out of this until the killer is behind bars." I reached up and touched the bandages on my cheek for emphasis. "These people play a little rough. I don't want to put you in danger."

Bledsoe's eyes widened. "No, I guess you're right."

"Don't worry, Ozzie. When the time comes, I'll see that you and the Howard Automobile Company get plenty of recognition for helping us out."

I headed north on Van Ness Avenue until one of the new Golden Gate Bridge signs directed me to turn left on Lombard. I stopped at the toll plaza and handed the smiling attendant a quarter, which entitled me to cross what Mayor Rossi described as the eighth wonder of the world.

Wonder or not, the span carried me safely to Marin County, where I followed U. S. Highway 101 past Sausalito and Mill Valley to the Corte Madera-Larkspur Wye. A few miles later, I was cruising up Magnolia Avenue through downtown Larkspur where, according to the Chamber of Commerce sign at the edge of town, "life begins."

Eleven

As towns go, Larkspur isn't much. It's a typical San Francisco suburban community of a few thousand souls, most of whom work elsewhere during the day and return from their daily toils at night for rest and relaxation.

Magnolia Avenue is Larkspur's main drag and the business district—a hodgepodge assortment of mostly one- and two-story wood-frame buildings—is loosely strung along it for a distance of four or five blocks. The town's predominant industries appeared to be dispensing booze and repairing cars. I passed at least four establishments dedicated to each of those enterprises. Of the remaining businesses, the most notable were the Blue Rock Hotel, the Larkspur Lumber Company, and a Northwestern Pacific train depot. What I did not see, however, was a dance pavilion called the Rose Bowl.

It was a quiet afternoon on Magnolia Avenue and I had no difficulty making a u-turn at its northern end. I retraced my route back through town with no better results. Finally I stopped at one of the few businesses showing any signs of life—the Larkspur Garage, just across a side street from Billy's Tavern—to ask directions.

An elderly mechanic in greasy gray coveralls was happy to oblige. He waved the wrench in his hand toward the side street and said, "The Rose Bowl is just up Cane here 'bout two blocks. Ya can't hardly miss it."

I thanked him and was turning to leave when he added, "But there ain't no sense goin' there now."

I turned back. "Why would that be?"

"'Cause it's all locked up. Ain't nobody ever there 'cept on Saturday nights."

"I see. Then where would I find the folks who run the place?"

He pointed the wrench over his shoulder and said, "Right next door here, at the fire station."

"The fire station?"

"Uh-huh. The volunteer fire department puts on the dances at the Rose Bowl."

I thanked him again and walked back to my car, half expecting the guy to stop me again and say there was no sense going to the fire station because there wouldn't be anybody there, either. He didn't, but since my Ford was already pointed up Cane Street, I decided to have a look at the Rose Bowl anyway.

Cane ran up a low hill and the Rose Bowl was on my left near the top, in the middle of a redwood grove that didn't seem to have any business being there. I couldn't see much from the street— just an entrance gate in an ornate lattice fence. A pair of glass ticket booths flanked the gate and a sign made of cut-out wooden letters floated in the tree tops above the entrance. It said, "WELCOME."

Besides a few Japanese lanterns hanging among the redwoods, there wasn't much more to see of the place. From all indications, the old mechanic was right—the Rose Bowl was deserted. Turning the Ford around just past some railroad tracks that ran along the eastern edge of the pavilion, I drove back down Cane Street and turned left onto Magnolia.

The fire station was between the Larkspur Garage and the City Hall. The Larkspur Volunteer Fire Department was housed in a California mission-style building of the sort that has become ubiquitous throughout the state. Two large arched doors stood open, revealing a pair of shiny red fire trucks.

One of the trucks was receiving some diligent polishing from a young blond-haired fellow in blue jeans and a mostly red plaid shirt. As I approached, he looked up, gave me a friendly sort of smile, and said, "Howdy, can I help you?"

"Hope so. I need to talk to somebody about the Rose Bowl."

"Well, you came to the right place. The guy who can tell you anything you want to know is right upstairs. I'll get him for you."

He walked over to a stairway and hollered up, "Hey, Cap! Somebody down here wants to see ya!"

The husky man in bib overalls who came down the stairs a few moments later had one of those cheerful rosy-cheeked faces that make you feel welcome even if you aren't. "Hi," he said, smiling from ear to ear, "I'm Cap Larson."

I shook the hand he offered and said, "Pleasure to meet you. I'm Parker Atkins."

Often that's all I need to say because a lot of people recognize my name. But Cap Larson just kept looking at me and smiling, so I added, "I broadcast the news on radio station KDG in San Francisco."

He cocked his head a little, then recognition dawned. "Oh, sure. I've heard of you. Don't listen to you, though. I like to hear the Wayne King orchestra and Gangbusters on KSFO."

Well, at least he didn't tell me how much he enjoyed my reports on all the misery in the world. I returned a reasonable facsimile of his smile and said, "I don't blame you. I'd be listening to Wayne King, too, if I could."

Larson nodded his understanding as if that made perfect sense to him, and asked, "What brings you all the way up to Larkspur, Mister Atkins?"

I fished the Chron article with Elaine Doherty's picture out of my pocket. "I came up here to do some background investigation for a story we're covering. I'd like to know if anybody saw this woman at the Rose Bowl last Saturday night."

Cap Larson took the clipping and stepped over to the open door where the light was better. "No, I don't recall seeing her, but that sure don't mean she wasn't here. We had twenty-seven-hundred-and-some at the Bowl Saturday night. I certainly didn't see 'em all."

The young fellow who'd been polishing the fire truck joined us and looked at Elaine's picture over Larson's shoulder. Larson held the clipping up for him. "What about you, Johnny? You remember this gal?"

"Nope, sure don't. But I was on the street patrol last Saturday. I didn't see many of the folks inside."

"Street patrol?"

Larson answered my question. "Oh, we get a few rowdy youngsters here from time to time, so the local folks like us to have a few of our volunteers out keeping an eye on the streets. Just to sort of discourage any problems."

I nodded. "Well, gentlemen, I appreciate your time."

The younger man gave me a wave on his way back to polishing the truck and Larson said, "Sorry we couldn't help. Say, you ever been out to one of our dances?"

"No, I can't say I have."

"Then you ought to bring a lady-friend and come on up. Only costs fifty cents a head and we use the proceeds to buy our equipment here." Larson gestured toward the nearest fire truck.

"Thanks. I might do that."

"If ya can, come on up this Saturday. We've got a new band coming in, Ernie Heckscher's orchestra. I hear they're real good."

I was nearly out to my car and bemoaning a wasted trip to Larkspur when a thought hit me. I turned around and went back into the station. Larson had gone back upstairs, but he wasn't the one I wanted to talk to.

The young man looked up from his polishing again and I said, "Just one more thing."

"Sure. What's that?"

"When you were out patrolling the streets Saturday night, by chance did you happen to see a white Oldsmobile convertible or a black Lincoln Zephyr . . . a new one?"

He didn't need to think about it for more than a second. "You know, I did see a Lincoln like that. And a white convertible, too. It could have been an Oldsmobile.

"I noticed 'em 'cause they were going way too fast out here on Magnolia. Like Cap said, a few of the kids get carried away sometimes. But most of 'em drive jalopies. I remember thinkin' this bunch must be some rich kids up here slummin'."

"Did you see either of the drivers?"

"Naw, I was clear up Cane Street. I only got a quick look at 'em when they shot through the intersection. But the second car was a Zephyr, for sure. Man, that's a swell car!"

"It sure is. Got any idea what time you saw them?"

"Gee, I can't say. It was after the firefall—that's the fireworks we set off at eleven—but I don't know how much later. It seems to me like it was a while, though . . . might've even been after midnight."

"That's close enough. Thanks, you've been a big help."

On the way out of Larkspur I thought about Larson's invitation to bring a lady-friend to the Rose Bowl and the fact that I didn't have one of those anymore. Dandy probably wouldn't have enjoyed slumming anyway.

I did another tour of the streets around Third and Market when I got back to the station about three-thirty. There were no black Buick Limiteds in the area. In fact, I hadn't seen one all day, but that didn't mean much because the killer hadn't wasted any time getting rid of the Lincoln. The Buick might just as easily be out of circulation by now. Especially if he'd damaged it badly enough getting out of the parking place in front of my apartment.

Charlie was typing furiously when I walked into the office. I said hello and she held up a hand, signaling me to wait a minute while she finished a thought.

There was another flurry of clacking and Charlie pulled the page out of her typewriter. "There. Hi, Park."

"Hi, yourself. Something break on the wire?"

Charlie slipped the page she'd just typed into the evening's script and said, "Uh-huh. Jean Harlow died this morning."

"No kidding? Who or what killed her?"

"It was uremic poisoning. She's been in the hospital for a couple of days. I guess Metro-Goldwyn-Mayer's been keeping it quiet."

Charlie actually looked a little sad about Harlow's death . . . like she was feeling some sort of personal loss. I wondered how many of our listeners would feel the same way when I read them the story. Personally, I couldn't remember ever seeing one of Harlow's films. Maybe I'd missed something.

"Park, I called Deputy Framm like you asked and told him about the Lincoln turning up."

"What did he say?"

"He sounded surprised, but I think he's still pretty angry with you. He said you'd better call him and be quick about it. What did you do to get him so riled up?"

"Darned if I know."

Charlie glared at me like she thought I was keeping secrets again and went off to the file room. I cranked a fresh sheet of paper into my typewriter and went to work on the crime report segment. It was done by the time Charlie got back.

She read through my three minutes of timeless prose and said, "Boy, you don't scare easily, do you?"

"What do you mean?"

"Well, if the killer was worried enough to take a shot at you after last night's story, this is really gonna get his dander up! You sure it's smart to go on with this?"

"No, it's probably not very smart at all, but our listeners will be hanging on every word. We got lucky last night when Osgood Bledsoe listened in. Maybe we'll get lucky again."

"Yes, and maybe the killer will get lucky tonight and blow your brains out. What does Dandy say about all this? She must be worried sick."

I sighed. "Dandy doesn't know anything about last night."

"You haven't told her about it?"

"I haven't told her anything. I haven't even seen her."

Charlie looked puzzled for a moment. Then she put it all together. "So that's what's been bothering you. You two have a falling out or something?"

"Charlie, it's time for you to go home. Go check the wire and get out of here."

"Okay, okay. It's none of my business. But I'll tell you this much, Mister Parker T. Atkins, that girl really loves you. If you don't patch things up with her, you'll be making a big mistake."

"Well, it won't be the first time . . . "

Charlie was already out the door. To hell with her. I picked up the evening's script and started through it.

A piece she'd done on J. P. Morgan needed a little editing. Morgan, it seemed, had told some reporters in his suite aboard the Queen Mary that doing everything one could to avoid paying income tax was every American's responsibility. Charlie's slant on the story definitely wasn't in keeping with KDG's conservative editorial leanings. Whether or not I agreed with her, it didn't seem wise to raise Kastner's blood pressure any higher than it already was. But then he probably wouldn't hear it anyway.

A few minutes before six, Dick Stewart and I played our nightly game of musical chairs in the announcers' booth. At six on the dot, I began telling San Francisco what was new. Charlie gave the Harlow story an emotional touch and I milked it for all it was worth, complete with dramatic pauses. Then, during the final commercial announcement, I turned the page to my crime report.

When the engineer cued me, I read, "KDG Special Crime Report—the murder of Elaine Doherty, Part Two. Monday night this reporter told you about the brutal, cold-blooded murder of a young woman named Elaine Doherty. It appears as if the cowardly villain responsible for her death was listening to that report along with the rest of you.

"He was lying in wait when your reporter arrived home last night . . . lurking in the shadows like the evil he personifies. Gunshots rang out, shattering the night air! His bullets came close, missing their mark by inches.

"Does that anger you, San Francisco? Does it make you mad that a reporter who brings the truth into your homes should be attacked in front of his own home?

"If it does, you may be able to help bring this thug to justice, just as a citizen came forward after last night's broadcast with information that led to our discovery of the murder car. That's right. The Lincoln that smashed into Elaine Doherty's young body out on Highway One early Sunday morning has been found. The San Mateo County Sheriff's Department is going over that vehicle with a fine-toothed comb at this very moment, cataloging the evidence that will help bring a vicious killer to justice.

"In the meantime, your reporter has uncovered more of Miss Doherty's tragic story. It is now known that a black Lincoln Zephyr was seen pursuing another vehicle matching the description of Elaine Doherty's car near the Rose Bowl dance pavilion in the Marin County community of Larkspur. That observation was made by a reliable witness sometime after eleven o'clock, Saturday night.

"Your reporter has also found further evidence suggesting that Elaine Doherty actually entered the Rose Bowl and spent some time there between ten and eleven p.m.

"Now, San Francisco, it's your turn. Elaine Doherty was approximately five-foot-four or five inches tall. She was of average weight for her height, with short brown hair and hazel eyes. Saturday night Miss Doherty was wearing a white silk jersey evening dress with a diamond teardrop pendant on a gold chain around her neck. The car she drove was a nineteen-thirty-six Oldsmobile convertible, white in color.

"If you were at the Rose Bowl Saturday night and saw Elaine Doherty, or if you saw an automobile like the one she was driving somewhere between Larkspur and the Daly City area after eleven p.m., you may have important information concerning her murder. Please call radio station KDG at Douglas two-two-two-four. That number again, Douglas two-two-two-four.

"And that's your news for Tuesday, June eighth. This is Parker T. Atkins. Goodnight, San Francisco."

Back in my office, I tossed the script on my desk and slumped into my chair amidst the usual squeaking. It was time to make the decision I'd been avoiding ever since visiting Dandy's empty office this morning. When I actually thought about it, the decision wasn't that tough to make.

Twelve

A maid I'd seen on previous visits answered my ring at the Harrisons' door. I asked to see Dandy. She said Miss Harrison wasn't in. I was asking if Dandy was expected soon and wondering if she was really out at all, when Samantha Harrison crossed the hall inside and saw me standing on her porch.

"Parker! How good to see you again. Please, come in."

She sounded as if she meant it, so I stepped past the maid and went in. Missus Harrison shook my hand with a firm grip and pointed me toward a chair in the sitting room. I felt awkward as hell. The only thing I could think of to say came out as an apology.

"I'm sorry for showing up unannounced. I was just hoping to catch Dandy."

Samantha Harrison's smile was warm with a wink in it. "And you were afraid that if you called ahead of time, she wouldn't see you. Right?"

"Well, I . . . ."

"Relax, Parker. Dandy and I had a long talk and a good cry together last night. I know the whole story."

Since Dandy couldn't very well tell her mother about our argument without saying what it was about, I realized Samantha Harrison must know all about my sordid past. It wasn't the sort of story mothers liked to hear about their daughters' gentlemen friends. I decided to state my business and get out of there.

"Missus Harrison, I shouldn't have blown up at Dandy the way I did. I feel badly about that and I just wanted to come by and talk it over with her."

"You should feel badly, Parker, but not for blowing up at Dandy. She had that coming."

That was wrong and I tried to tell her so. "No, she didn't. I lost my . . . ."

"Parker, hush up a minute and listen to me. Dandy is every bit as much to blame for the difficulty you two are having as you are. The root of the problem is that you have not been talking to each other."

I was starting to get a little hot under the collar. "Missus Harrison, Dandy and I have talked until we're blue in the face. She just doesn't see . . . "

"She doesn't see what? That you are a hopeless drunk? That you aren't worth spit and you never will be?"

That did it. I started to get up.

"Parker, sit down! I put Dandy through the wringer last night and she managed to stand it. So, by heavens, you can, too!"

I sat.

"That's better. I know it isn't easy to sit there and listen to an old battle-ax tell you things you don't want to hear, but it's high time you heard them from somebody. Parker, the reason you can't convince Dandy that you are hopeless and worthless is that you are neither. Oh, I know you have had some hard times. I also know you have the courage and convictions to overcome them. I know that, and Dandy knows that. The problem is, you don't know it."

"I know it. I'm the guy who's doing it."

"Then stop feeling sorry for yourself and start liking the man you see in the mirror every morning. If you got to know him, you would discover he is really a very likeable person.

"Just look at what you've accomplished. Sure, you got yourself into a jam, but you also managed to get out of it. And now you have one of the most popular radio shows in San Francisco. If you can convince all those people who listen to you every night that you are worth something, you ought to be able to convince yourself. Isn't that so?"

"But it's not that easy. There are a lot of things . . . ."

"Of course it isn't easy. It is terribly difficult to believe in yourself again when you feel you have failed at something important. It will take a great deal of effort to regain your confidence. Still, the proof that you deserve that confidence is all around you."

Samantha Harrison shook her head as if amazed. "It is really ironic that you think yourself unworthy of Dandy."

"I don't see the irony in that."

"The ironic part is Dandy thinks she doesn't deserve you. Last night she sat here calling herself a spoiled brat because she has never had to face life the way you have. In her eyes you are a knight in shining armor."

I couldn't help smiling. "You're right. That's pretty ironic."

"Parker, I'm going to be blunt."

It seemed to me she'd already been about as blunt as a person could be, but Samantha Harrison proved me wrong.

"I am going to ask you a straight question and I want a straight answer. Do you love my daughter?"

"Well, that depends on . . . ."

"Do not flim-flam me, young man. I want a yes-or-no answer. Do you love Dandy or not?"

"Yes, I love her. But after yesterday . . . ."

"Parker, I asked Dandy the same question last night and got exactly the same answer. Yesterday just proves you two have some problems to resolve. And the way you resolve those problems is by discussing them honestly. You must stop feeling sorry for yourself and tell Dandy exactly what you think. And you must listen to her as well. Do that, and be willing to meet each other halfway and there is no problem the two of you cannot solve.

"I know my daughter and I believe I have you sized up pretty well. You and Dandy are at a fork in the road. If you take the wrong turn, you will leave something behind that only comes along once in a lifetime. Take it from an old woman who learned her lessons the hard way. If you do not try just as hard as you can to work this out, you will always regret it."

She paused a moment and smiled. "Alright, Parker, the sermon is over. I hope you understand why I had to speak my mind."

I nodded. "I understand. And you're right. I guess I needed a good slap in the face to see it."

Samantha Harrison turned in her chair and looked up at a large ornate clock above the fireplace. "Goodness, look at the time."

I glanced at my wristwatch. It was almost eight. "Were you expecting Dandy by now?"

"Yes. She and Gladys Doherty went uptown to do some shopping and have dinner. It's one of those things women do to cheer each other up. Heaven knows they both needed it."

"Well, I should be going."

"You are certainly welcome to wait here for her. I promise to keep my opinions to myself for the rest of the evening."

Grinning, I said, "Leaving has nothing to do with your opinions. In fact, I have a lot of respect for those opinions. But it's been a very long day and last night was a very long night."

"I heard your broadcast, so I wasn't surprised by your appearance. I doubt if Dandy heard it, though. If she had she would have been burning up the telephone wires trying to find you."

"I wish she was. I really want to talk with her. There's something else, too. I won't be at home tonight. I'm staying at an auto court for a few days until things calm down. If I leave the phone number with you, will you please give it to Dandy when she comes in and ask her to call me?"

"Of course I will." She got up and walked over to a small writing table. Uncapping a fountain pen, she said, "Where are you staying?"

"At the Mission Auto Court." I dug a card out of my wallet and read off the number. "It's Randolph five-eight-five-eight."

After repeating the number to be sure she had it right, Samantha Harrison came over and gave my hand a squeeze. "Parker, you go on and get some rest now. I will give Dandy your message and I know she'll call you the minute she comes home. And don't worry. Things are not so bad that they cannot be mended."

"Thanks to you."

She took my arm and saw me to the door. We said goodnight and I looked around cautiously as I walked down the steps. There were no black sedans parked on the street and there were no gunmen lurking in the shadows.

My drive to the Mission Auto Court took about forty-five minutes because I made two stops--one for a tankful of gasoline and the other for some Chinese take-out. When I got there, I checked with the night clerk. There were no messages.

Hanging up my jacket, I slipped the Colt into the pocket of my slacks. I thought about taking a bath, but settled for washing my hands and the parts of my face that weren't covered by gauze and tape.

Sitting on the bed eating my chow mein and fried rice, I listened to the last half of the Jack Dempsey program on KGO. He was followed at nine by the Chron's Ted Powell doing a sports commentary. At nine-thirty Johnny O'Brien came on with fifteen minutes of harmonica music. At nine-forty the telephone finally rang.

"Hello?"

"Parker, this is Samantha Harrison. I'm sorry to be a bother, but Dandy isn't home yet and I am becoming concerned."

Something hot fluttered in my stomach. "Did you call the Dohertys'? Maybe she . . . ."

"I have already called them. Gladys isn't home either. I cannot imagine why they would be out this late."

I could. My imagination was working just fine and the hot thing in my gut was growing by leaps and bounds.

"I'm not sure what to do. Bernard, Dandy's father, is in Los Angeles   and   .   .   .   ."

"You did the right thing, Missus Harrison. I'll be there in half an hour, unless you can think of anywhere I can look for Dandy on the way."

"I don't know. The stores will all be closed by now. They might have gone to Lucca's for dinner. They go there sometimes."

"How did they go downtown? By car?"

"Yes, Gladys came by the house and picked Dandy up in that open car . . . the white one."

"Alright, Missus Harrison. I'll swing by Lucca's first, and then I'll come to your place. I shouldn't be more than forty-five minutes."

Transferring the Colt back to my right coat pocket, I headed out the door. Driving in on Mission, I tried to ignore what my stomach was telling me and listen to my head instead. The news there wasn't any better.

Of course, my biggest fear was that Elaine Doherty's killer or killers—it was seeming likely that more than one person was involved—might have developed an interest in Gladys. Without knowing why they killed Elaine in the first place, it was certainly a possibility I had to consider. If that was the case and Dandy was with her when they showed up . . . . I decided not to dwell on the consequences of that situation.

On the other hand, the girls might have just decided to take in a movie. Neither my head nor my gut was buying that one.

Lucca's Restaurant is out in North Beach at Powell and Francisco so I cut over to Market and turned north on Powell. I made good time because the traffic was light and the signals cooperated. Even so, it was ten-thirty when I got there. Lucca's was dark.

I spiraled out over a three block radius from the restaurant looking for Gladys' Oldsmobile among the parked cars. When that proved fruitless, I took Lombard over to Buchanan and pulled into the Harrisons' circular drive.

Samantha Harrison was at the front door before I got up the steps. Her expression told me Dandy still wasn't home.

"Should we call the police, Parker?"

"That might be a good idea, but I want to make another call first. May I use your telephone?"

"Certainly. There is an extension in the library."

"What's the Dohertys' exchange?"

"Bayview three-one-six-six. But I spoke with Rutherford earlier, before I called you. The girls weren't there."

"It's not Rutherford I want to talk to."

I dialed B-A-three-one-six-six and someone answered on the first ring. The voice was unmistakably that of Jacob Doherty. He sounded anxious.

"Yes, who's calling?"

Suddenly I knew for a fact that what my stomach had been telling for the past hour was right. "Doherty, this is Parker Atkins. I want to know what's going on and I want to know right now."

"I'll handle this Atkins. It's none of your affair. You just stay the hell off this line!"

The phone clicked in my ear and I slammed it down hard. "Damn!"

"Parker, what's the matter?"

"Missus Harrison, who answered the phone when you called the Dohertys' earlier?"

She thought briefly. "Their houseman. Why?"

That was the answer I expected. I nodded and said, "I don't want to alarm you, but I'm pretty sure Dandy and Gladys are in trouble."

"What sort of trouble?"

"I don't know yet, but I'm certain Jacob Doherty knows what's happened to them. I'm going over to ask him some questions."

"And you want me to stay here?"

"I think that would be best. Do you know Police Chief Clayborne?"

"Yes. His wife and I serve on some charity committees together."

"Good. If you don't hear from me within an hour, call Clayborne. Talk to him directly. Tell him your daughter and Gladys Doherty are missing and you think their disappearance is connected to Elaine Doherty's murder."

"Oh, no!"

"Try to stay calm, Missus Harrison. You and I are going to get Dandy out of this in one piece, but we'll need our wits about us to do it."

Thirteen

It took me less than five minutes to drive from the Harrisons' to the Dohertys', and in that time I decided how to handle Jacob Doherty. The plan would probably get me charged with assault and a few other felonies, but if my theory was right, it was the only way to find the answers I needed in time to get Dandy and Gladys out of this alive. If it wasn't too late already.

I had to be careful, though, because my theory was based on a pretty ragged chain of logic held together mostly by guesses and hunches. The first link in that chain consisted of the only logical reason I could think of for Elaine Doherty's murder. As a rule, big guys in Lincolns don't go around killing good little rich girls just for grins. There had to be a motive. And the most likely motive I could think of was that Elaine had become some sort of threat to the killer. She knew something the guy in the Lincoln or his boss didn't want anyone else to know.

But what did Elaine know that got her killed? Probably the same thing that panicked Gladys when she realized I was going to broadcast my story about Elaine being murdered. Jacob Doherty was in on the secret, too. He was willing to pay a great deal of money and commit a murder to keep a lid on whatever it was.

So the Dohertys had a big secret and lots of money, the two primary ingredients for blackmail. Except blackmailers seldom kill their victims. It's bad form. If you kill your victim, there's no one left to pay off. In fact, the only reason a blackmailer kills his victim is if the victim becomes a threat.

That figured to be why Elaine was murdered. Somebody was blackmailing the Dohertys—or at least Elaine—and she threatened them with the cops. If I was right and the killers were greedy or desperate enough, they would think of another way to get their hands on the Doherty money . . . like kidnapping Gladys.

It would certainly explain why Jacob Doherty was answering his own phone instead of letting his houseman do it. It would also account for him picking up on the first ring and being insistent about keeping his line clear. That had to be it. Doherty had heard from the kidnappers within the last hour, and now he was waiting for ransom instructions.

If I was right, even if Jacob Doherty met their ransom demand, the kidnappers were going to kill Dandy and Gladys anyway. Why not? They had already killed Elaine, and since you can only go to the electric chair once, why leave witnesses behind?

That meant I had to find the girls fast. To do that I needed to know what Jacob Doherty knew; but first, I had to get past his houseman, Alec. Previous experience told me Alec wasn't someone you got past easily, so the situation called for drastic measures.

After parking in the Dohertys' drive, I got a pair of handcuffs left over from my cop days out of the tool box in my trunk. Then I took a deep breath and went to do what I had to do.

As big and tough as he was, Alec never had a chance. He opened the front door about eighteen inches so he could tell me to go away. My right foot hit the door so hard the knob jerked out of Alec's hand and he was left scrambling for balance. I leaned forward, came down on my right leg and kicked him square in the groin with my left foot.

Alec's eyes glazed for a second before he doubled over in pain. I stepped around him, grabbed the back of his shirt collar and drove the top of his head into the hardwood door frame. Alec hit the floor limp, like an oversized sack of dirty laundry.

I checked for a pulse and was relieved to find he still had one. Closing the door, I slid him across the foyer and cuffed his wrists around a beautifully hand-carved banister post that looked sturdy enough to keep Alec out of my hair when he woke up.

If memory served me right, there was a desk in the library with a telephone on it. That seemed like a logical place to start looking for Jacob. One of the library doors was ajar, and as I approached, Jacob Doherty's voice came through it loud and clear.

"Alec! Who the hell was at the door?"

I walked in with my hand in my jacket pocket and said, "It was only me, Jake."

He was sitting right where I'd pictured him, behind the desk. His gray eyes went wide and he grabbed at one of the desk drawers. I casually pulled the Colt out of my pocket and pointed at his face.

"Forget it, Jake. You'll never make it."

Doherty looked down the barrel of my Colt and gave up on the desk drawer. I moved closer and told him to stand up. He reached for a gold-handled cane that was leaning against the desk.

"Leave the cane there. Use the desk for support if you need it."

He glared at me, but leaned on the desk and, with some effort, stood up. I used my foot to push his chair around the end of the desk where he couldn't reach any drawers and motioned for him to sit down again.

He sat, and while I opened the drawer he'd been fumbling with, Doherty said, "You're making a big mistake, Atkins. You have no idea what you're doing!"

I lifted a heavy old Colt Navy thirty-eight caliber revolver from the drawer. "I know exactly what I'm doing, Jake."

Putting my Colt away, I flipped his open and dumped six brass rounds into a metal wastepaper basket at my end of the desk. In Doherty's quiet library, the clatter was louder than I expected.

"My granddaughter's life is at stake. You may have killed her just by coming here!"

I tossed his empty revolver back into the drawer. "Jake, at this point I don't really care much about you or your granddaughter. Someone else has been caught up in your rotten little problem and she's the only one I'm interested in."

He looked confused. "What? Who are you talking about?"

"I'm talking about Danielle Harrison."

"What the devil does the Harrison girl have to do with any of this?"

"She was with Gladys when your granddaughter was snatched tonight."

Doherty cocked his head and looked at me suspiciously. "How do you know Gladys was taken? How do you know anything about any of this?"

"I'm not answering questions tonight, Jake, you are. Who else is in the house?"

"There's just me and Alec. How the devil did you get past him?"

"Where are your son and his wife?"

"I sent them to the Saint Francis Hotel for the night. I couldn't stand any more of their whining."

"Good. Then you and I won't have any distractions until the kidnappers call back. What time are they supposed to call?"

"Before midnight. But I demand that you tell me how you know my granddaughter was kidnapped."

"Just good guesswork, Jake. But that doesn't really matter. Last night you tried to buy my help. Tonight, you get it whether you want it or not. And I suggest you want it, because I'm just about your only hope of ever seeing Gladys alive again."

"No! All you're going to do is get her killed. They may be watching my house. If they've seen you . . . ."

"Jake, use your head. You could give them every penny you've got and it wouldn't make one iota of difference. They aren't going to turn Gladys and Dandy loose."

Doherty's eyes narrowed. "What do you mean?"

I sat in a wing chair near the fireplace where I could watch both Doherty and the door. "These people have already killed once. Or have you forgotten about Elaine already?"

"No, damn your eyes! I haven't forgotten anything."

"Then figure it out. Why should they leave witnesses behind? Murder and kidnapping are both capital offenses."

He thought about it and I watched reality sink in. Jake started shaking his head back and forth slowly as if he couldn't believe what was happening and it occurred to me that this was probably the first time in a good many years that someone had him over a barrel. With Jacob Doherty, things were usually the other way around.

"Doherty, the only way we're going to get those girls out alive is by going after them. And I can't do that until you tell me the whole story."

After focusing several seconds' worth of hateful glare in my direction, he sighed. "Alright. We'll do it your way. It all started a few months back when Gladys told me she was pregnant. She came to me instead of my son and his wife because she knew they would make a big fuss and insist that she marry the young man."

"And you didn't?"

He looked surprised. "Of course not. Why should one little mistake ruin her whole life?"

"So you arranged an abortion?"

"Yes. Alec made some discrete inquires and found a doctor who runs a sanitarium up in Mill Valley. It cost a hell of a lot of money, but this doctor was supposed to take care of Gladys' problem anonymously and quietly."

"Didn't work out that way, huh?"

"Oh, he took care of the problem, alright. Alec drove us up there early one morning and we were back by the middle of the afternoon. Then, a few weeks later, Gladys came to me in tears with some photographs. She'd gotten them in the mail, along with a note demanding fifty thousand dollars or copies of the pictures would be sent to every newspaper in town."

"What was in the photos?"

Doherty made a face. "They were disgusting. The first one showed us walking into the sanitarium." He closed his eyes and shook his head. "The rest were taken during the operation."

"When did the photos show up?"

"Gladys got them last Friday and brought them to me on Saturday."

"What did you do with the pictures and the note?"

"They're in my safe at the office."

"How did they set up the payoff?"

"Gladys was supposed to meet someone on the old wooden footbridge across Stow Lake in Golden Gate Park Tuesday morning. They were to give her the film negatives and all of the other prints they had in exchange for the money."

"And you went along with that?"

"Not right away. It galled me that those scalawags thought they could get away with such a thing. But I'd never seen Gladys so upset. She believed they would do what they said and cause a scandal that would ruin her life forever. Gladys kept begging me to pay them and I finally gave in. Then they killed Elaine."

I'd guessed right about the blackmail—I just had the wrong victim. Still, Elaine was dead, not Gladys. That just didn't make any sense.

I said, "Are you sure the blackmailers killed Elaine?"

"I wasn't at first. I didn't even know she was involved. We just thought Elaine's death was a terrible accident."

"Then Gladys told me you thought Elaine had been murdered. I still didn't see the connection until Gladys admitted that Elaine had come across the pictures Friday night and demanded to know what was going on.

"Somehow she must have talked to the blackmailers and threatened to call the cops if they didn't leave Gladys alone. That's the only way I can figure it."

"Does that sound to you like something Elaine would do?"

Doherty nodded grimly. "I'm afraid Elaine inherited my stubbornness and then some."

"I take it you didn't make the payoff this morning?"

"Hell, no! I got the money, but after I knew they'd killed Elaine, I damn well wasn't going to give them any of it. Besides, I didn't think they'd have the nerve to show up."

I pictured the stack of hundreds Doherty had shoved across his desk at me and wondered if it was part of the payoff money. That made me wonder about something else.

"Last night you offered me a lot of dough to find Elaine's killer before the cops did. What made you think I could?"

"Because I could tell you where to start looking. The police don't know anything about the blackmail racket. I figured that would give you all the head start you needed."

I hoped to hell he was right about the head start and looked at my watch. It was already twenty to twelve.

"Alright, Jake, we'll get back to that in a minute. When did you first hear from the kidnappers?"

"A man called about ten-thirty. He said they had Gladys and wanted a hundred thousand dollars or they would kill her. He told me he'd call back before midnight with instructions about when and where I was supposed to leave the money."

"Alright, I need the rest of the details from you, but I have to make a telephone call first. I'll keep it short."

He started to object, then clamped his mouth shut and swept an arm toward the telephone. I dialed and Samantha Harrison answered on the first ring.

"Hello, Missus Harrison. This is Parker. I need to be very brief for the moment, but the situation is this. Gladys Doherty has been kidnapped. Dandy was most likely taken with her. I'm working on a way to get them back, but I need a little more time. Can you stand waiting another half hour?"

Her words were tense, but direct. "I can and will. Is there anything I can do in the meantime?"

"No, nothing until we talk."

"Very well, I will expect you in half an hour."

I hung up and turned to Doherty. He looked drained. I said, "Jake, there are two things you need to do above all else when the kidnappers call back."

Doherty's mind was somewhere else. He jumped a little when I said his name. "What? Oh. What are they?"

"First, delay the payoff for as long as possible. No matter when they want the money, tell them it will take longer. Number two; insist on proof that Gladys and Dandy are alive. Say you have to see them, or at least speak to them, before anybody gets a dime. Tell them for all you know the girls may already be dead."

82

He winced a little at the last part, but nodded.

"If you can do those two things, you'll greatly improve our chances of getting the girls back. And understand that Dandy is part of this deal."

"I understand and I'll . . . ."

The crash that interrupted Doherty came from somewhere toward the front of the house. I pulled the Colt out of my pocket and stepped quickly to the library door. My guess was that Alec had come around and found a way to break free of the banister post.

I leaned cautiously into the hall and saw nothing. Stepping through the library door and hugging the wall, I started toward the foyer. Another twenty feet brought me to where the hall turned and opened into the entry. I went around the corner quickly, ready to shoot anything that moved.

There was nothing to shoot. The only things out of place were a piece of oak banister that had been pried up from the post and the front door, which was standing open. Had Alec really cut and run or was the door open just to make me think he had?

I stepped cautiously out onto the porch and looked up and down Buchanan Street. Sure enough, there was Alec down the block, running toward Pacific Avenue. Apparently he wasn't quite as devoted to Captain Doherty as I'd thought. Since I couldn't think of any good reason to go after him, I closed the door and headed back to the library.

Just outside the door, I heard Doherty's voice. Inside, I found him on the phone. The kidnappers had called, and judging from his end of the conversation, Doherty was handling them pretty well.

"Threats don't change the facts. The earliest I can possibly raise that much money is late tomorrow afternoon and that's that."

He looked at me and nodded with an expression that said the kidnapper was buying his story. Doherty listened a moment longer and spoke into the receiver again.

"That's all fine and good, but you aren't going to see a penny of that money until I have absolute proof that both Gladys and her friend are still alive. For all I know, you've already killed them."

He listened again for a few seconds. "No, that won't do. I demand to see them or, at the very least, talk to them before we go any further."

A moment later Doherty looked up and nodded again. "That's better. Alright, I'll expect your call at five o'clock tomorrow afternoon, but I want you to call me at my office, not here."

He interrupted another short pause, saying, "I don't give a damn what you like or don't like. My private office number is Douglas three-seven-one-nine. If you want to do business, that's where I'll be at five tomorrow afternoon."

Jake listened once more, then hung up the phone and sagged back into his chair as if the conversation had used up the very last of his strength.

I said, "It sounds like you handled that very well."

"It was easier than I thought it would be. At first he wanted the money by ten tomorrow morning. I told him I . . . well, you heard that part. Now they expect me to get the money by five. He said they'd have Gladys and Danielle there to talk to me when he calls back with the ransom delivery instructions. That's the best I could do."

"That's more than I'd hoped for. But I'm pretty sure we're dealing with amateurs so that gives us a slight advantage."

"I hope it's enough."

With more optimism than I felt, I said, "It will be when you give me a few more details to work with."

I was opening my notebook when Doherty suddenly remembered the crash we'd heard. "What the devil was that racket a minute ago?"

"Oh, I left Alec handcuffed out in your foyer. The noise was him breaking the banister loose so he could get free."

"Well, where the hell is he now?"

"Last I saw of him, he was hot-footing it down Buchanan toward Pacific."

Doherty's eyes narrowed in an expression that was somewhere between suspicion and disbelief. I nodded in agreement with what I thought was going through his head and said, "Yeah, that surprised me, too."

I pulled a pencil out of my inside coat pocket and said, "Alright, do you know the doctor's name?"

For the second time I saw him force his thoughts back to the here and now. "No, I never knew it. I don't think Alec knew it, either, but his clinic is called Twin Oaks Sanitarium. It's up near Mill Valley. You take One-Oh-One to the town of Almonte and turn left on State Highway One. You go through a little business district and turn right on Almonte Boulevard. The sanitarium is at two hundred Almonte, at the corner of Rosemont. It's a big wooden building with a lot of windows overlooking a slough off of Richardson Bay. The place looks more like a large house than a business."

I finished copying his instructions. "Did you see the doctor?"

"No. The only ones I saw there were a woman at the front desk and a man in a white coat. It was the kind of coat doctors wear, but the woman called him an orderly."

"What did they look like?"

"The woman was nice looking with sort of red-brown hair. The man was big . . . as big as Alec. And he had a very square jaw, almost like a character from the funny papers. I think his hair was dark brown. He didn't look like he belonged there. For one thing, his coat was too tight. A real employee would have had a coat that fit."

There was no question about who played the role of the orderly. I'd seen him in two other performances. On those occasions he was playing a killer.

"Is anybody shown in the blackmail photos besides you and Gladys?"

"No, just us and I'm only in the first one."

"Alright. Can you think of anything else about all this that would help?"

Doherty was obviously tired. He rubbed his forehead and said, "No. Not at the moment."

"Okay, I'll get busy and check with you by noon. Where will you be?"

He looked around the library with something like distaste and said, "I'll be at the office. Douglas three-seven-one-nine."

"Fine. I'll call you there."

As I started for the door, Doherty said, "Wait a minute, Atkins. What about the money? Should I get it ready or not?"

I thought about his question for a moment. "I don't know, Jake. That decision is up to you. But if it was me and I could lay my hands on that much, I'd probably get it ready—just in case."

It was twelve-twenty-five when Samantha Harrison met me at her front door for the third time that night. I gave her a complete account of my conversation with Jake Doherty. I did not, however, mention my encounter with Alec. When I was done, she asked the same question I would have asked.

"Parker, what are Dandy's chances?"

"Right now, I'd say they're pretty good. Doherty made it clear to these people that they wouldn't get any money until he had proof that both of the girls were okay. They seemed to accept that. So my guess is they're still okay."

She nodded and said, "I don't suppose there is any need to tell you that I'm frightened out of my wits over this. Are you sure we shouldn't notify the police?"

"Well, the police are already involved to the extent that the San Mateo County Sheriff's Department is looking for Elaine's murderer and the San Francisco Police are looking for the same man in connection with the shooting last night.

"So far, all the Sheriff's Department has on the case they've gotten from me. Also, this thing has spread out over three counties now. I don't think we have time to wait while three different police agencies sort out who has jurisdiction over what. Just the same, you certainly have a right to call Chief Clayborne and ask for an investigation."

Samantha Harrison studied me intently for a long time. "Parker, at the moment I'm feeling completely helpless. That is an unusual feeling for me and I do not like it. My only daughter is in grave danger and I desperately want to do something to help her. So I'm going to do exactly what Dandy would want me to do. I'm placing my full faith and confidence in your judgment and ability. Now, please go and bring Dandy home."

I told her I would do my best and that she would hear from me by noon. Samantha wished me luck and I pointed my Ford south toward the Mission Auto Court.

Fourteen

2:00 A.M.—Wednesday—June 9, 1937

After showering, changing the bandages on my face, and getting into some clothes that didn't look quite so much like I'd slept in them, I felt almost human again. I completed the refurbishing of Parker Atkins by walking across Mission Boulevard to an all-night doughnut shop and ordering two glazed with a cup of stale, black coffee that had the consistency of old motor oil.

Munching the doughnuts at a sticky table next to a fly-specked window, I leafed through the pages of my notebook and tried to assemble the Doherty puzzle. Most of the pieces fit pretty well, but there were a few that didn't line up like they should.

One of the pieces that didn't quite fit was the collection of photos that arrived with the blackmail demand. I could see how a picture of Gladys and Jacob arriving at the sanitarium might have been snapped without their knowledge, but the pictures taken during the operation were another matter. Gladys should have been awake throughout the entire procedure. How could pictures be taken without her knowing about it?

Then there was the matter of the sanitarium itself. The doctor had to have some connection with the place or he couldn't perform abortions there. That connection should make him fairly easy to find, so the blackmailers had to be very confident that Doherty wouldn't go to the cops. Of course, it was possible that the doctor wasn't in on the blackmail scheme. But how could the pictures have been taken if he wasn't?

Leaving that vicious circle, I considered another piece of the puzzle that was out of kilter. The note and the photos arrived in the mail last Friday, but the blackmailers gave Gladys until Tuesday to make the payoff. Even if they were allowing for a delay in mail delivery, four days is a long time to let someone think about whether they're going to cough up fifty grand or call the cops. They certainly weren't showing the same patience with their ransom demand.

Thinking about the puzzle pieces that didn't quite fit brought another question to mind. How did Elaine contact the blackmailers and set up her meeting with them Saturday night? Did she just call Twin Oaks Sanitarium and ask to speak to the head of obstetrics and blackmail? Somebody told her how to reach the blackmailers and that somebody had to be one of two people, either Gladys or Alec.

Okay, there were some flaws in the story. I could sort them out later. Right now all that mattered was finding Dandy. I imagined her in a dark room somewhere, scared out of her wits. She didn't belong in that picture.

Swallowing the dregs of my muddy coffee, I fished some change out of my pocket and went outside to a telephone booth next to the doughnut shop. I dialed "O" and asked for long distance. When the operator came on, I gave her Framm's number at the San Bruno sub-station of the San Mateo Sheriff's Department. It was time to bite the bullet.

The guy on the desk said, "Yeah, Sergeant Framm is on tonight, but he's out on a call."

"Do you expect to hear from him soon?"

"Oh, probably sometime in the next half hour. You want to leave a message?"

"Yes. Is there an all-night coffee shop in San Bruno?"

"Huh? Oh, sure. Sandy's . . . right on the El Camino at Euclid, a block north of San Bruno Avenue. Why?"

"Tell Will that Parker Atkins called and I'll meet him at Sandy's around . . . ," I looked at my watch, "three-thirty."

"Okay, I'll tell him, but I can't guarantee he'll be there."

"I'll take my chances on that. Thanks."

I walked back to the auto court and checked with the night man again. There were no calls, so I climbed into my Ford and followed Mission Boulevard south through Daly City. A few miles later Mission became the El Camino Real, which took me past the cemeteries of Colma. Driving by those endless rows of moonlit tombstones rekindled the hot thing burning in my stomach. A lot was riding on the shoulders of Dandy's knight in shining armor.

Sandy's coffee shop was easy to find. A giant pink neon coffee cup marked the spot. There were no sheriffs' cars in the parking lot, but I was a few minutes early.

Inside, the dazzling light provided by a multitude of overhead fixtures gleamed and sparkled on chrome and maroon plastic. Sandy's wasn't exactly doing a land office business at that hour, so I had my choice of booths. I picked one near the entrance and ordered a glass of freshly squeezed orange juice that came out of a machine behind the counter.

I'd hardly tasted my juice when a pair of headlights swept through the parking lot. They belonged to a black Ford sedan with white doors. I watched Framm park next to my Ford and get out of his cruiser. As he walked toward Sandy's entrance, we made eye contact through the window. I nodded and he just stared back at me. This wasn't going to be any fun at all.

Framm tossed his uniform cap on the table and slid into the booth. "Atkins, I have half a mind to slap the cuffs on you and haul your butt right down to the county jail!"

"Good morning to you, too, Will." My attempt to keep the conversation light fell on deaf ears.

"Why the hell haven't you returned any of my telephone calls?"

"Well, I've been a little busy." I almost added, "doing your job for you," but I managed to resist that temptation.

"I'll say you have . . . busy lousing up a criminal investigation. And from the looks of your face, I'm not the only one who's been wanting to take a poke at you."

"That's true, Will. You're in good company. In fact, I'm pretty sure you'd like to meet the guy who did this."

"Why?"

At least I'd peaked his curiosity. "Because he's the same guy who killed Elaine Doherty. He took a couple of shots at me Monday night."

"Oh yeah, I heard your broadcast last night. I heard you Monday night, too. I also heard from Jacob Doherty. You aren't very popular with him, either. He said I should arrest you for harassing his granddaughter."

"He's singing a little different tune now. I just left him a couple of hours ago."

"Oh? And now I suppose he's your biggest fan."

"I wouldn't say that, but he's sure anxious as hell for me to find his other granddaughter before she's murdered, too."

Now I really had his attention. "What in blue blazes are you talking about? Who wants to kill Gladys Doherty?"

"The guys who kidnapped her."

"What? Gladys Doherty's been kidnapped? When the hell did that happen?"

I looked at my watch. "Six or seven hours ago. She was taken with another woman, Dandy Harrison, sometime before ten last night by the same people who killed Elaine."

"Damn! How come SFPD didn't notify me? We're supposed to be cooperating on this thing!"

"They didn't tell you about the kidnapping because they don't know about it yet."

Will threw both hands up like a traffic cop halting cars in an intersection and said, "Stop right there. I think you'd better back up and give me all this from the beginning."

"That's why I asked you to meet me here."

The waitress interrupted us at that point to take Framm's order for a cup of coffee. I waited until she returned a moment later with a Silex coffee pot. When she'd finished pouring nearly equal amounts of the hot brown stuff in Will's cup and on the table, I began my story.

"After I spoke with you on the phone Monday, I talked to Gladys Doherty at her home. That was mostly a wasted effort because, even though I'm pretty sure she knows what went on Saturday night, she wasn't talking. All I learned was that something or someone is scaring the hell out of her."

"Yeah, I saw her later in the afternoon with the same results. Her lies weren't even very good."

"One piece of information turned up while I was at the Dohertys', though. The Oldsmobile was there and I took a look at it. I found a ticket stub from the Rose Bowl dance pavilion in Larkspur down behind the front seat. The date stamped on it was June fourth."

Framm smiled a little for the first time. "Yeah, I know. I found it, too."

"Actually, I was surprised to see the Olds there. How come you didn't impound it Sunday morning so your crime lab boys could go over it?"

He shook his head in disgust. "I gave orders for the car to be towed in. I was as surprised to see it in the Dohertys' driveway as you were. Turns out the family made arrangements to have the car picked up and their guy got to it before ours did.

"By the time I discovered it at the Dohertys', about the only thing I could do was go over the car myself. You didn't remove anything from it did you?"

I put on a shocked expression. "Heavens, Will, that would be against the law, wouldn't it? Tampering with evidence and interfering with a police investigation?"

"Alright, alright. Go on."

While I was telling him about my conversation with Jacob Doherty Monday night, he got his notebook out and made notes. The proposition Doherty offered me surprised Framm. I couldn't tell from the expression on his face whether he believed me or not. When I got to the shooting incident at my apartment, Will stopped me.

"Now, there you're in trouble. The sergeant working on the shooting called me after your broadcast tonight. He was mad as a hornet about you not sticking around to talk to them . . . thought I might know where to find you. You sure it was the same guy you saw out on the coast highway?"

"Yup. Either him or his twin brother."

He made another note or two in his book and said, "Okay, go on."

I told him how Osgood Bledsoe's call led me to the Lincoln and he said, "Now, that car we've got. The lab boys started on it yesterday afternoon."

"They find anything yet?"

"They sure have, some bits of white thread stuck in behind the smashed chrome headlight ring. They're a perfect match with Elaine Doherty's dress."

I got my own notebook out and started making notes of my own. "Good. Anything else?"

"Not so far. Somebody cleaned that Lincoln up pretty well, outside and in, before they took it to the Buick dealership. We were lucky they missed the threads."

"What about the registration? Did you track down North Bay Therapeutic Enterprises?"

"Yes, that came in late yesterday—Tuesday—afternoon. I started a background check on the owner, Doctor Donald Davis. About all I have so far is that he used to have a permit to operate a convalescent hospital in Mill Valley . . . "

"The Twin Oaks Sanitarium?"

Framm tossed his notebook on the table and glared at me. "Why the hell do I bother?"

"You said Davis 'used to have' a permit to operate the place? He doesn't anymore?"

His eyebrows raised a notch or two. "Oh, so there's actually something about this case you don't know?"

I shrugged and grinned. "Maybe a few little details."

Framm looked a little happier. "Yes, his permit to run the place expired on May thirty-first and he never applied for renewal. According to the Board of Health, the place has been shut down ever since."

That was bad news. It meant I wasn't going to walk into the sanitarium and find the kidnappers standing around waiting for me. My disappointment must have shown because Framm said, "What's the matter? Does that mean something?"

I told him I'd get to that in a second and picked up the story with my visit to Larkspur. He opened his notebook again and jotted down what I told him about the Larkspur volunteer fireman seeing the Lincoln and a white convertible Saturday night.

"So the fireman is the witness you mentioned in your broadcast? It probably wouldn't mean much in court, but his statement and the ticket stub add up to a pretty safe bet that Elaine Doherty was at the Rose Bowl Saturday night. But that isn't exactly the sort of place you'd expect to find a society gal like her, so why was she there?"

"My guess is she met the blackmailers there and was trying to get them to leave Gladys alone."

This time Framm threw his pencil on the table. Leaning back, he let out a long exasperated sigh. "What blackmailers, for heaven's sake?"

I related my most recent conversation with Jacob Doherty in its entirety, beginning with Gladys' announcement of her pregnancy and ending with the kidnappers' second telephone call. Framm made a lot more notes in his book, and when I finally finished, he shook his head in disbelief.

He said, "It sounds like the Doherty family has its own private crime wave going on up there. Murder, an illegal abortion, blackmail, and now kidnapping. Who's this other gal who was nabbed with Gladys?"

I took a deep breath and said, "She's just a friend of Gladys' who was in the wrong place at the wrong time."

He looked at me for a long moment, then said, "Do I detect a hint of personal involvement here?"

"Yeah, very astute of you."

"Let me ask you something. How sure are you that the kidnappers are the same people who killed Elaine and blackmailed Gladys?"

"Pretty sure. Jacob Doherty's description of the sanitarium orderly matches the guy who killed Elaine and traded the Lincoln.

I suppose it's possible somebody else kidnapped Gladys and Dandy, but what are the odds of a coincidence like that?"

He shook his head. "Not good. It just strikes me that, after their blackmail scheme fell apart and they'd committed murder, these characters have a hell of a lot of nerve turning around and kidnapping Gladys Doherty."

"Uh-huh. They are either very greedy or desperate. Or both."

Framm looked at his watch. "Well, Park, you've got just about twelve-and-a-half hours until the kidnappers call Doherty. What are you going to do now?"

"I've been wondering the same thing myself. I guess I'll start by going up to Mill Valley and taking a look at that sanitarium. After that . . . ." I shrugged.

"You want some company?"

I wasn't expecting that and Framm took my surprised expression to mean something else. He held up his hands in a defensive gesture. "Okay. Sorry. I just thought I'd offer."

Shaking my head, I said, "No, Will. You've got me wrong. I'd be very grateful for your help. I'm just surprised."

Framm looked frustrated. "Park, I've been trying to work this thing long distance while you've been right in the middle of it. It's about time I did something useful. Besides, a little help might come in handy because we're dealing with at least one pretty tough customer here. I know you haven't seen much proof of it so far, but I'm really a pretty good cop."

"I know you are, Will. And I'd be glad to have you along. When does your shift end?"

"With the hours I've been working, any time I want. I just have to go by the station and drop the patrol car off. After that, you can follow me over to my place. I'll change out of this uniform and tell my wife what I'm up to. Then I'm all yours."

Paying our check, I wondered if Framm was telling me the real reason he offered to join me on my sojourn to Mill Valley. Maybe he just wanted to keep an eye on me so I didn't louse up his case any worse than I already had. Then one of my old man's favorite expressions came to mind. Never look a gift horse in the mouth.

Fifteen

The sky beyond the hills above Tiburon was just beginning to lighten as Will Framm and I pulled into the sanitarium's gravel parking area. I shut the Ford's engine off, and we sat there in the early morning silence staring up at the dark building and deciding what to do next.

Built on the lower slopes of a hill, the sprawling redwood structure overlooked the slough where Highway 101 crosses an arm of San Francisco Bay known as Richardson Bay. We could see the headlights of the morning's first commuters moving toward The City along the highway below us. It was only five-thirty.

The view was bound to be spectacular when the sun came up, and the sanitarium's architect designed the place to take advantage of that feature. Two narrow wings were built at right angles to each other, one to the west and one to the north of a square central structure with a set of double doors that looked to be the main entrance.

Halfway up the walk from the parking lot to the entrance doors there was a low redwood sign supported by two posts. My headlights illuminated the sign when we pulled in. It showed two oak trees separated by the words, "Twin Oaks Sanitarium."

I glanced over at Framm. "What do you think?"

"I'd say the place is empty, just like it's supposed to be."

"Any suggestions?"

"Nope. We're two counties away from my jurisdiction, so you'd better call the plays."

Leaning over, I took my old beat-up flashlight from under the seat and said, "Well, you may want to drive back to that coffee shop we passed on the way in and kill a little time."

"You plan on breaking in?"

I opened my door and said, "That's the idea."

Framm opened his door and muttered, "Well, take your damn keys. We don't want somebody stealing our car while we're up there breaking and entering."

I couldn't help chuckling. "Ya know, Will, you're alright for a cop."

"Thanks a lot."

The hardwood entrance doors were locked up tight, and the dead bolt securing them looked like it would be tough to pick. I suggested we hike around the wing to our left and look for an easier way in.

As we walked, I pointed my flashlight beam at a few windows. The curtains were all drawn tight. The next door we came to was at the end of the west wing. There were four small windowpanes set in the upper half of the door. I put my flashlight up to the glass and looked in at an empty corridor with a linoleum floor.

Framm shook his head. "This won't work either. The lock is on the inside . . . no way to pick it."

"Then we'll just have to get in the hard way."

I glanced over my shoulder to make sure we couldn't be seen from any of the houses on the hillside behind us. The coast looked clear, so I rapped the butt-end of my flashlight sharply against the glass pane closest to the doorknob. The broken glass made a little racket when it hit the floor inside, but not enough to worry about.

Avoiding the jagged edges, I reached in and snapped the lock off. Opening the door, I made an "after you" gesture with my arm and followed Framm inside. The scraping sounds made by our shoes grinding the broken glass against the linoleum had the same affect as fingernails on a blackboard.

There were six rooms in the wing, three on each side of the central corridor. They all looked identical and contained exactly the same things . . . four bare walls around a straight-back wooden chair, a nightstand, and a metal bed frame with no mattress.

We found the mattresses a few minutes later. They were stacked on the other side of a door that led from the corridor to the sanitarium's central section. Actually, we found twelve mattresses, which probably meant the rooms along the other corridor were identical to the ones we'd just seen.

The space we were in looked like a lobby or reception area. It held a small desk and some furniture that seemed like the sort people sat on while they were waiting for someone or something. I pictured Jacob Doherty sitting in one of those chairs.

When a quick search of the desk revealed nothing, we turned our attention to the doors that led to and from the lobby. There were several. Besides the one we'd just come through, there were the double entry doors we'd seen from the car, another door in the east wall, and two more in the north wall.

Framm opened the door in the east wall and found a rest room. I tried the north wall door closest to the wing we'd already explored and found a storeroom with another door at its far end. I knew it was a storeroom because the walls were lined with shelves from floor to ceiling. They were all empty.

I shined my flashlight beam around the floor and found a small pile of dust and debris in one corner, as though someone had swept the room without bothering to pick up the sweepings. We looked through the pile. It held nothing more interesting than a crumpled toilet paper wrapper.

Framm looked through the door in the far wall of the storeroom. It opened into a commercial kitchen of the kind you might find in a small restaurant. There was a double sink, a six-burner gas stove, and an oversized refrigerator. The rest of the space was taken up by counters, with cupboards above and below.

We made quick work of the cupboards. Old Mother Hubbard would have felt right at home. The refrigerator was also empty. A second door in the same wall as the door we'd just come through revealed a walk-in pantry. The pantry shelves were empty, too.

We found another pile of sweepings in one corner of the kitchen. It contained only the sort of rubbish you'd expect from any kitchen that had just been thoroughly cleaned.

The remaining door was in the east wall of the kitchen, and beyond it we found an area that reminded me of a hospital nursing station. It had a counter and the space behind it included a small room that contained some locked storage cabinets with glass doors.

Framm said, "This must have been where they stored patient medications. I don't think they'd leave anything of interest in here."

He was right. Neither the drug room nor the nursing station revealed so much as a scrap of paper. A door alongside the counter led to the second wing which looked identical to the first.

Splitting up, Framm headed off up the north wing and I went the opposite way, down a short corridor with a few more doors to explore. Since he had the flashlight, I used my cigarette lighter to cut through the gloom.

A room behind the first door on my left appeared to be an office. The flickering flame from my lighter dimly lit a desk and some wooden filing cabinets. This room definitely called for a more thorough inspection with the flashlight.

The door on my right revealed another bathroom. I was opening up the last door on the left side of the hall when Framm showed up.

"That wing's the same as the first one. You find anything?"

"Well, there's another bathroom across the hall, and the other room on this side is an office. Point that light in here."

The flashlight beam showed us an examination table, a counter and some cabinets. I said, "This must be where the good doctor performed his abortions."

We went over the room as thoroughly as my flashlight allowed and, once again, found absolutely nothing. One thing was clear, though. If this is where the blackmail photos were made and Gladys was awake, there was no way they could have been taken without her knowledge.

The door at the end of the short hall opened back into the lobby, so we returned to the office. We went over everything in the room with no better results than we'd had anywhere else in the sanitarium, and I was pretty much giving up hope of finding something that would help us locate Dandy and Gladys.

That's when Framm said, "Oh oh. Here's a little something they missed."

I moved quickly to the desk he'd been searching. "What'd you find?"

"A couple of receipts under the bottom desk drawer. They must have slipped out of the drawer and ended up in the space underneath it."

"Let's see."

He laid the wrinkled scraps of paper out on the desk so we could examine them. The first receipt was dated May twelfth and came from Tompkin's General Store in Reed, California. The neatly hand-printed list of items purchased included one bottle of Parker Brothers ink (blue), one package of Gillette razor blades, one bottle of LePage's mucilage, and a quart of Kleines' peppermint schnapps.

I looked at Framm. "Peppermint schnapps?"

"That's what it says."

The second receipt was issued by the Hildebrand Dry Cleaning and Laundry Service of San Rafael on May eighteenth. It showed that the amount of two dollars was received for the washing and pressing of four white work coats.

The last receipt was also from Tompkin's General Store. It recorded the purchase of a twelve exposure roll of Eastman Kodak film and another bottle of Kleine's peppermint schnapps on May twenty-first.

Framm asked, "When did Gladys Doherty come here for her abortion?"

"I didn't get the exact date, but the timing sounds about right. Who do you suppose developed the film for them? They couldn't just take something like that down to the corner drugstore."

"They may have developed it and made the prints themselves. It's not hard. In fact, I used to do it myself in a little darkroom I set up in my garage."

"I also wonder how many bottles of Kleines' schnapps this general store sells."

"Good question. We could ask them if we knew where the town of Reed was."

"Well, if it's around here, I've got a map in the car that should tell us."

I folded the receipts and slipped them into my wallet. Then we left the Twin Oaks Sanitarium the way we'd entered it, through the west wing.

We walked out of the gloom into a brightly lit world of brilliant blues and dazzling greens. The freshly-risen sun sparkled on Richardson Bay and on the chrome bumpers of the cars crawling south along Highway 101.

In the Ford, I rummaged through the glove compartment and came up with a Flying A road map of San Francisco and the bay region. An examination of the Marin County section showed us that the community of Reed was just across the highway and a little north of the sanitarium.

That surprised Framm. "Son of a gun! I've lived within thirty miles of here all my life, and I never heard of Reed before."

"Sounds like the sort of place where if you blinked driving through it you'd miss it entirely. I wonder what time Tompkin's General Store opens."

"It's about seven now, and we're not far away. I guess it wouldn't hurt to go take a look."

I nodded and started the Ford's engine. Seven o'clock. Ten hours before Jacob Doherty would hear from the kidnappers . . . ten hours until Dandy and Gladys outlived their usefulness. There have been times in my life when ten hours seemed like an eternity.

Right now, with as little as we had to go on, it didn't seem like nearly long enough to find two very tiny needles in a gigantic haystack.

Sixteen

We followed Almonte Boulevard north around the sloughs to Tiburon Boulevard. There we turned east and crossed the highway to where the map said we would find the wide spot in the road known as Reed. It was there alright.

Finding Tompkin's General Store was even easier. It was a white wood-frame building that comprised a full third of Reed's business district. The other two-thirds consisted of a little two-pump Shell service station and a tavern called the Strawberry Point Inn.

There were a dozen older houses scattered around among eucalyptus trees . . . all of them wood-frame and painted white like the store. A few of the yards had lawns and flower beds, but much of Reed's landscaping was left to the whims of nature. And for the most part, nature was doing a pretty good job. Just a few rusty automobile parts and broken-down household appliances were still visible through the weeds.

Parking in downtown Reed was a relatively simple matter. I just pulled off in the dirt between Tompkin's front porch and the road. I figured it was legal because someone had already parked an old beat-up Studebaker pickup truck there. Up on the porch, a small neatly painted wooden sign hanging next to the screen door said, "Closed," but there were lights on inside.

Framm said, "Looks like somebody's in there. How do you want to handle this?"

"Well, since we don't have to break in this time, it might be better to rely on your badge than on my charming personality."

He shot me a wry look that conveyed his whole-hearted agreement with that suggestion, and we got out of the Ford. My knock got an almost immediate response. An elderly gent wearing a clean white canvas bib-apron and thick wire-frame glasses opened up and peered out at us through the screen door.

Framm flashed his tin and said, "Morning. Are you the owner?"

The old guy squinted at Framm's badge for a moment before answering. "Yup, sure am. You fellas are a little out of your bailiwick, ain't ya?"

Given the thickness of his glasses, I was surprised he could see Framm's shield well enough through the screen door to read "San Mateo County." It didn't matter. Framm had an answer for him.

"We're looking into something that happened down in our neck of the woods, and it seems to involve some folks from up here. Mind if we ask you a few questions?"

"Nope, don't mind at all. Come on in."

He unhooked the screen door, and we walked into another time. Tompkin's was an authentic turn-of-the-century general store right down to the worn wooden floor and jars of penny candy on the counter next to an ornate brass cash register. The only things missing were a pot-bellied stove and a checker board, and they probably would have been there, too, except there wasn't any room for them. The place was jammed to the rafters with merchandise, some of which looked as though it had passed from new to antique without ever moving from its spot on the shelf.

At the back counter, Framm made the introductions. "I'm Deputy Will Framm of the San Mateo County Sheriff's Department, and this is Park Atkins."

With a hearty handshake for each of us, the old gent said, "Pleased to make your acquaintance. I'm Ed Tompkin. Bought this place from old man Brier back in ought-seven." Tompkin seemed to see some irony in what he'd said. He added, "'Course, now I'm an old man, too. But you fellas didn't come here to listen to ancient history, did ya?"

"To tell the truth," Framm said politely, "the history we're interested in at the moment is a little more recent. We have a couple of receipts from your store, and we'd like you to tell us whatever you can about the folks you gave them to."

I took the two Tompkin's receipts out of my wallet and spread them on the counter. He held each of them up to the light for a careful examination.

When he was done, Tompkin said, "No doubt about who I gave those to. It was Missus Davis."

"Missus Davis?"

"Yup. Her husband is Doctor Davis. Ran that sanitarium over to the other side of the highway."

Framm smiled. "You've got a pretty sharp memory, Mister Tompkin. What makes you so sure it was Missus Davis?"

"The peppermint schnapps. How many folks you know drink that awful stuff? Not many, I venture. Well, there ain't but one person in these parts that drank it, either.

"'Bout a year ago, Missus Davis comes in here and asks if I ever heard of Kleines' peppermint schnapps. Turns out they had an old gal at the sanitarium who'd been drinkin' the stuff for forty years and got down right orn'ry if she couldn't have it.

"Well, the only place they could get that brand was down in Frisco. Missus Davis wanted to know if I would stock it so they didn't have to go so far to keep this old gal happy.

"Said I'd try, and I did. Kleine's is made in Germany and I have to get it from an importer clear back in Pennsylvania. You can see the doggone stuff costs an arm and a leg. But that didn't seem to matter. Missus Davis came in every two weeks, regular as clockwork, to pick up a new bottle. Still got three bottles from the last order left on the shelf. Now the sanitarium is closed, I guess they'll just sit around gathering dust like everything else in this place."

I now knew much more about Kleines' schnapps than I ever cared to know. What I wanted to do was grab the old man by his collar and shake Davis' address out of him. But I knew Framm was handling Tompkin exactly right, so I kept my mouth shut and let the deputy do his job.

"Mister Tompkin, why do you suppose Missus Davis came to you for the schnapps rather than going to one of the bigger stores over in Mill Valley?"

"No mystery 'bout that. Missus Davis and her husband live 'round here, so it was easy for 'em to stop in and pick up whatever they needed on their way home from the sanitarium."

"By chance, do you know their address?"

"Nope, she never has said, and I don't never see 'em 'round 'cept when they stop by here. Can't be too far away, though. Maybe down to Belvedere or Tiburon. Lots of well-to-do folks buyin' places down that way lately."

"Is Doctor Davis well-to-do, Mister Tompkin?"

"I'd say so. I mean, the missus is always dressed up real nice, and they drive a big, fancy automobile and all."

"What sort of car do they drive?"

"Don't know as I can tell you the kind. They just got a new one, though. Used to come by in a big dark blue sedan. Then, a few weeks back, they showed up in a black one. Real sleek-lookin' job."

"Can you describe Doctor Davis and his wife?"

"Can't say much about the doctor. Don't recall that he actually ever came in the store. Always sent the missus in. So I've only seen him through the window. Remember thinkin' he looked sort of young for a doctor, though. And his hair is kinda light colored."

"What about Missus Davis?"

Tompkin lit up like a Christmas tree. "Now, her, I can describe. A real pretty one, she is. Has a real friendly smile and green eyes. My missus, rest her soul, had green eyes. Missus Davis' hair is sort of reddish brown and all curly. Lot of them rich women dye their hair, but I don't think she does."

"How tall would you say Missus Davis is?"

"'Bout up to here."

Tompkin held his hand up about nose high, which made the woman five-three or four. Framm added that to the notes he'd been making in his book.

"Anything else you can think of?"

"'Bout Missus Davis? No, I . . . . Yes, by gum, there is somethin' else. She has a little mole . . . nowadays they call 'em beauty marks . . . right here above her lip."

Tompkin pointed to a spot on the right side of his face, and Framm added the location of Missus Davis' mole to his notes. While he wrote, I asked a question of my own.

"Ed, have you ever seen anybody else with Missus Davis?"

He shook his head. "No, sir. In fact, the doctor hasn't even been with her lately. I always see Missus Davis to the door and the last two or three times she's stopped in, she was drivin' that big black machine all by herself."

"When did Missus Davis come in last?"

Tompkin looked thoughtful for a moment. "Have to say it was the middle of last week. Maybe Wednesday or Thursday."

Framm looked at me and said, "Anything else you can think of, Park?"

I shook my head and he turned back to Tompkin. "Ed, you've been very helpful. Just one more thing. We'd appreciate it if you wouldn't mention our visit if you should happen to see Missus Davis in the next day or two."

We'd obviously raised Tompkin's curiosity, but he seemed reluctant to come right out and ask the obvious. Instead, he said, "Happy to oblige. I surely hope that pretty young gal and her husband ain't in no sort of trouble."

Framm handled it well. "Oh, I don't think there's anything to be concerned about. It's probably just a misunderstanding. That's why we'd like to finish looking into things without upsetting anybody. That okay with you?"

"Sure. Mum's the word."

Tompkin looked relieved. Missus Davis was clearly one of his favorite customers, and he might have warned her about our visit if he thought she was in trouble. He still might, but there was nothing more we could do about that.

As I pointed the Ford north on Highway 101, Framm asked, "Where are we headed?"

"Mostly, away from here."

"Why?"

"Elaine's killer—the orderly, or whoever he is—knows me and he knows this car. If he sees us out here, they'd know we were closing in, and somebody might panic."

"Are we?"

I glanced over at him. "Are we what?"

"Closing in?"

"I sure hope so. I didn't really expect to find them at the sanitarium. Davis would know that's the first place anybody would look. That's why they cleaned the place out so thoroughly when they left. But if Davis has a residence around here, they might figure it was a safe place to keep the girls."

"Yes, but only if it can't easily be connected to the sanitarium. That could make them difficult to find. I mean, they aren't likely to be in the telephone book."

"Maybe. On the other hand, they may not be that smart. I have a feeling that Davis is an amateur who's in way over his head. He's probably been doing pretty well with the abortions and a little blackmail from time to time. Compared to kidnapping, that was relatively safe because his clients weren't likely to make a fuss."

"I see your point, but would an amateur have killed Elaine?"

"Probably not, and I don't believe he ever intended to kill her. My guess is things got out of hand. In fact, Davis may not have had anything to do with the murder directly. I think he just meant for the big guy with the cartoon jaw to bring her back. The guy may have panicked when he saw me out there and decided running her over was the quickest way to solve the problem.

Remember, there was only one guy in that Lincoln. Davis wasn't even there."

"Okay, I can buy all that, but wouldn't an amateur have cut and run when he found out about Elaine's murder? If your theory about Davis being an amateur is right, would he have the nerve to turn around and kidnap Gladys?"

"That's where we're missing a piece of the puzzle. Somewhere there's another player in this game who's been influencing Davis . . . somebody greedy enough or just plain nervy enough to risk being caught. It might be the guy who killed Elaine, or it might even be Davis' wife. At this point, I just don't know."

"But you're still certain Davis is behind the kidnapping?"

"I'm almost positive. It's possible Davis isn't running the show anymore, but I can't believe anyone else just happened to get the bright idea of kidnapping Gladys Doherty at this exact moment."

Framm didn't say anything for a long moment. When he did his voice was solemn. "What if you're wrong?"

It was a good question and there was only one answer. "Then we will have wasted what little time we had, and two more women will very likely be dead."

He sighed. "Well, for what it's worth, I think we're on the right track. Besides, it's the only track we've got. So what's next?"

"First, I need to find a pay phone and call the station to let my assistant know what's going on. It's getting close to eight."

The first public telephone we spotted was next to a service station at the south end of San Rafael. I dialed the operator and placed a long distance call to Douglas two-two-two-four. After depositing two dimes and a nickel, I heard the KDG switchboard operator come on the line. I asked for Charlie.

Charlie must have been at her desk because she answered right away. "Park, where are you?"

"In San Rafael. Listen, there's a better-than-even chance I won't be back in time for the broadcast tonight. Get a hold of Dick Stewart and tell him he'll have to sit in for me. Write something into the script about me being away on a special assignment or words to that effect. Got it?"

"I got it, but what's going on?"

"I'll tell you in a second. Were there any telephone calls about last night's broadcast?"

"Yes, but most of them were just moral support. I didn't find anything in the stack that looked useful."

"Okay. Grab your pencil and a pad. Here's what's going on."

"Alright. Shoot."

"Gladys Doherty was kidnapped last night, and Dandy happened to be with her at the time. They took Dandy, too."

"Oh no! Is Dandy alright?"

"She's probably scared as hell, but I think they're both safe for the moment." I gave Charlie a rundown on my conversation with Jacob Doherty and what Framm had found out about Davis. I also told her how we'd found Tompkin and what we'd learned from him.

"I have it all, Park."

"Good. Keep it to yourself unless something happens to me."

"Oh, great! What am I supposed to do if something happens to you?"

"Write the hottest damned news story of your career."

That remark was followed by a whole bunch of silence. Finally I said, "Don't worry, kiddo. Nothing's going to happen to me. Hell, I've got one of San Mateo County's finest along for protection."

"Park, just find Dandy and get her out alive. Okay?"

"That's what I plan to do."

Charlie said she'd take care of everything at that end, and we hung up. I left the booth and found Framm inside the service station office with a local telephone directory. His expression told me he'd been right about not finding Davis in the phone book.

I said, "No listing for Doctor Donald Davis, huh?"

"Nope. Figured it was worth a try, though."

I nodded. "You need to make any calls before we go?"

Framm looked at his wristwatch. "No, not yet. It's only eight-fifteen. There won't be anything new from my background check on Davis until later."

"Okay. In the meantime, let's find Hildebrand's Cleaners and see if they can add anything to what we know about Davis. Then we can try the county recorder's office. Maybe the good doctor has bought himself a piece of property somewhere in these parts."

Seventeen

Compared to the other Marin County communities I'd visited in the past two days, San Rafael was a metropolis. It was even big enough to have an old part of town. That's where Hildebrand's Dry Cleaning and Laundry Service was—next door to a paint store in the four hundred block of Fourth Street. Their old wooden building looked as if it might have already been there when Sir Francis Drake showed up here back in fifteen-hundred-something.

Inside Hildebrand's you could've sliced the hot, humid air with a knife, and the din beneath the cloying fog would have been right at home in a boiler works. Most of the racket came from several steam pressing machines which were also responsible for the heat and humidity. The rest of the noise was generated by a dozen Orientals who were operating the equipment and chattering at the top of their voices to be heard over the hissing and clanking.

A middle-aged Chinese woman greeted us at the front counter and promptly forgot what little broken English she spoke when Framm displayed his badge. In fact, the whole place suddenly got several decibels quieter. I wondered how many of Hildebrand's employees would end up on a slow boat back to China if we'd been immigration cops.

Framm tried his best to put her at ease, but she wasn't having any of it. I laid the receipt from the sanitarium on the counter, pointed to it, and asked if she remembered the customer.

She looked at it briefly and shook her heard vigorously. "No remember. Long time past. No remember."

"Does anyone else here speak English?"

"No speakee English. No remember."

Framm looked at me and said, "I guess we could come back with the immigration authorities. Some of those guys speak Chinese."

He emphasized "immigration," and she clearly recognized the word. Her eyes started twitching back and forth between us.

I answered quietly, "No, Will. We've already ruined her day. Let's get out of here."

He looked relieved and nodded. I thanked the woman and she looked relieved, too.

We passed the ancient Marin County courthouse on our way to the dry cleaners, and as I retraced the route that would take us back there, Framm said, "I wonder how long it's been since anybody named Hildebrand owned that place."

"Could be Hildebrand still owns it. Maybe he just found a way to increase profits with cheap labor."

"It wouldn't be the first time."

The county recorder's office was on the first floor of the old courthouse building which, according to a plaque near the entrance, was built in 1873. The clerk who met us at the counter was considerably younger than the courthouse and eager to help. It only took a few moments to discover that Donald Davis was not a property owner in Marin County. Checking a little further, we learned that the only parcel owned by North Bay Therapeutic Enterprises was the one on which Twin Oaks Sanitarium was situated. The clerk even checked North Bay's deed to see if it showed an address other than the Post Office box we already had. It did not. All of which added up to one very disappointing dead end.

Back in my Ford, Framm asked the obvious question. "Where to now, Park?"

Shrugging, I said, "I really don't know. If you've got any bright ideas, now would be a good time to trot one out."

"Afraid I'm fresh out of bright ideas. I could sure use some breakfast, though. How 'bout we stop and do some thinking over a plate of scrambled eggs?"

It was as good an idea as any, especially since I'd been running on a couple of glazed doughnuts for the last six hours. I stopped at an eatery a few blocks from the courthouse and we ordered breakfast.

I brought the Flying A map in with me, and while we were waiting for our food, I refolded it so we could study the Marin County area without taking up the entire table. I looked at Tiburon Boulevard, the only road of any significance that past near

Reed and Tompkin's store. It consisted of two loops. The northern loop began at Highway 101, passed by Reed, and circled around to meet the highway again a little further north in Corte Madera. The southern loop was longer and circumnavigated the hilly peninsula that divided Richardson Bay from the main body of San Francisco Bay. The only communities accessible by Tiburon Boulevard's southern loop were Tiburon and Belvedere.

After studying the map with me for several minutes, Framm said, "If Tompkin's is on the Davis' route to and from the sanitarium, they probably live somewhere on this peninsula. We might try to find the sheriff's deputies who patrol the area and ask if they know Davis or remember seeing either the Lincoln or the Buick. It's a long shot, but it might pay off."

"Except for one thing. They'd want to know why we were asking. We'd either have to involve them or lie, neither of which is a particularly appealing option."

"Well, we might be able to borrow another car somewhere— one that wouldn't be recognized—and do our own looking, but that's a lot of ground to cover. Unless we happened to spot the Buick, we could drive right by them and never know it."

"True," I agreed. "And for all we know, the Buick has gone the way of the Lincoln by now."

Our breakfasts arrived and I continued to ponder the question of what to do next. The clock was ticking, but I wasn't. The Davises were the only lead I had and I wasn't doing a very good job of following it. That thought was still bouncing around in my head when Framm finished eating and looked at his watch.

"It's almost ten. Think I'll use that pay phone back there to call in and see if my inquiries on Davis have gotten any results yet."

Framm was gone a good ten minutes. When he returned, his notebook was out.

"Got a little something back. A Doctor Donald Davis was practicing in Phoenix, Arizona, up until about fourteen months ago. That's when the state medical board suspended his license to practice medicine. Care to guess why?"

"Illegal abortions?"

"Alleged illegal abortions," he corrected. "Davis' license was suspended pending an investigation, but he left the state and the matter was dropped."

"Convenient."

"Yeah, isn't it? That's all I've got so far. Oh, and the Arizona authorities confirm that Davis is married. His wife is a registered nurse, and she was implicated in the charges against him."

The flimsy edge of an idea flickered through my brain. "Will, did they give you Mary Davis' maiden name?"

"Uh-huh. Her full legal name is," he checked his notes, "Mary Trevor Davis."

I nodded. "Let's go back to the courthouse and ask the clerk to see if Mary Trevor shows up on his list."

"You think Davis might have recorded the deed in his wife's former name?"

"It's a possibility."

The helpful clerk was still behind the counter, and he even seemed happy to see us again. I asked him to check the records for the name Mary Trevor and we hit the jackpot.

"Yes, we have a Mary Trevor listed. I'll get the deed and we'll see where her property is located."

I took a deep breath and looked at Framm. He raised his eyebrows and looked hopeful.

The clerk came back a few minutes later with the deed and a plat map. Rolling the map out on his counter, the clerk checked some numbers and said, "It looks like . . . yes. The property owned by Mary Trevor is out on Strawberry Point. Right here."

His finger was on a point of land that extended into Richardson Bay from the north. Specifically, he was pointing at an inlet that appeared to be almost due east and directly across Highway 101 from the sanitarium.

I said, "Do you have another map of the area you could spare, one we could mark that location on and take with us?"

"Sure, I think I can find something for you. Be right back."

This time the clerk returned with a smaller map bearing the name of the Loftus Real Estate Company. "This outfit gave us a bunch of these maps. It isn't very precise, but it should help you find the place. Let's see . . . ." He referred to the plat map, then put a pencil dot on the real estate map.

"If you fellows want to take a look at the place, go south on the highway to Tiburon Boulevard and turn east. Then you take this trail—I don't think it has a name—to the right. The turnoff is right here, just east of the highway. That's all hills and marshes in through there, but you might be able to drive all the way to the property. Especially if somebody lives there."

As we headed back down 101, Framm asked the same question I was pondering. "What do you think? Did we hit pay dirt?"

"Well, the name matches, and the location sounds good. If the Davises really live on that property, Tompkin's General Store wouldn't be directly on their route to the sanitarium, but it isn't far off."

"From the plat map, it looks like the property is fairly isolated. How would we get there without being seen?"

"I don't know about actually getting there, but I think I know how we can take a look at the place. From the scale of that map, Richardson Bay is less than half a mile across there. I'll pull off the highway down here a ways, and we can take a look from this side of the bay."

We passed Tiburon Boulevard, the sanitarium, and State Highway One before I found what I was looking for. After making an extremely illegal left turn across the highway, I pulled off and parked near the Northwestern Pacific's railroad tracks. The binoculars in my trunk were only six power, but they'd have to do.

Framm and I hiked across the tracks and down a weed-covered slope to the water's edge. We were below the highway, and the only signs of life were some sea gulls and a couple of old-timers fishing about thirty yards down the shoreline. They waved a greeting, which Framm returned while I focused the binoculars on Strawberry Point.

According to my map, the inlet I was looking for was formed by two small peninsulas that jutted out near the point where Highway 101 crossed Richardson Bay. In fact, some of the pilings that supported the highway bridge were sunk into the northern peninsula.

I almost missed it because most of the two-story house was hidden behind a row of tall eucalyptus trees growing along the property's western edge. About all you could see was the roof and part of one wall. The house was down close to the water. There was a hill directly behind it and what appeared to be a dirt road winding down the hill. About the only other feature I could make out was a short dock with a skiff tied to it in front of the house.

I handed the glasses to Framm and said, "Look toward that row of dark colored trees. The house is behind them."

"I've got it. Boy, if that's where the Davises are holed up, they picked themselves a great spot, didn't they? Nice and isolated with a good view of the only road in."

Seeing the skiff tied up in front of the place was giving me an idea. I said, "But that road isn't the only way in."

Framm lowered the binoculars. "What have you got in mind?"

"How do you feel about some fishing?"

"You mean we get ourselves a boat and cruise right by their front door?"

"Exactly."

"I wouldn't mind a little fishing. Wonder where we can find a boat."

"I don't know, but I'll bet those fellows do."

He glanced over at the two fishermen. "I'll bet you're right."

I was right. The old guys happily gave us the name of their favorite bait shop where we could not only rent a boat, we could also rent some tackle to go with it. It was a place called Bay Bait and Tackle and it was just a few miles to the south, in Waldo. They said to be sure and ask for their pal, Al. He owned the shop.

Eighteen

It wasn't hard to imagine what Kastner would say when he saw my expense reimbursement claim for the fifteen bucks' worth of boat and fishing tackle Framm was busy renting. I was also thinking it was a darn good thing Framm turned out to be a fishing enthusiast because Al, the owner of Bay Bait and Tackle, would have spotted me for a phony right off. Everything I know about fish I learned from the menu at Bernstein's Grotto up on Powell Street.

While Framm loaded our newly acquired gear into the boat, I excused myself to make three calls from a booth outside the tavern next door. The first was to Samantha Harrison.

"Hello Parker. Do you have any news of Dandy yet?"

"I'm making progress, Missus Harrison. And I have some help. Will Framm, the deputy from San Mateo who's been investigating Elaine Doherty's murder volunteered to give me some unofficial help."

"May I ask what you have learned so far?"

"The most important thing is that we've located a house owned by the doctor who tried to blackmail the Dohertys and who I believe kidnapped Gladys and Dandy. It's in an isolated spot on Richardson Bay and the girls may be there. We're on our way to look it over right now."

"What will you do if Dandy is there?"

"To be honest, Missus Harrison, I don't know. I'm playing this strictly by ear. I won't know what I can do until I see what's there."

"I understand. Is there anything I can do from here?"

"For the moment, just keep your fingers crossed for luck. I'll call you again as soon as I have something to report. Okay?"

"Alright, Parker. Be very careful."

My second call was to Charlie. She didn't sound nearly as cool and collected as Samantha Harrison.

"My god, Park, I've been worried out of my mind! Have you found Dandy yet?"

"Not yet, but I think we're close. We've traced a piece of property out on Strawberry Point in Richardson Bay to Davis. The deed is in his wife's maiden name, Mary Trevor. You getting this down?"

"I'm getting it, Park. Is that Trevor, t-r-e-v-o-r?"

"Yes. Will and I are taking a boat over there to look at the house."

"A boat?"

"It's the only way we can get close to the place without being noticed."

"You think Dandy and the Doherty girl are there?"

"I hope so. If they aren't, I have no idea where to look next. Anything new at that end?"

"I talked to Dick Stewart. He'll do your broadcast. Otherwise, there's nothing going on here."

"Okay. I'll call again as soon as I learn something. Stick close to the phone, just in case."

"Will do. Park, be . . . ."

"I know, I'll be careful."

My last call was to Jacob Doherty. I gave the long distance operator his private office number and he answered on the second ring.

"Yes?"

"Jake, this is Park Atkins."

"What have you found out, Atkins?"

I gave him a quick report on our morning's activities. I also asked if he'd heard anything new. He hadn't, but he used the opportunity to take some of his frustration out on me. Doherty wasn't in control and he didn't like it.

"Listen, Atkins, don't louse this up. You bullied me into letting you handle this last night, so I'm holding you personally responsible for my granddaughter's safety. If anything happens to her . . . ."

"You got the ransom money, Jake?"

"I got it, but . . . ."

"Have you heard from your man, Alec?"

"No."

I had another question for him. He wasn't going to like it, but the pieces of this puzzle that didn't fit right were still nagging at me.

"Okay, one more thing. I need to know something about what's shown in those blackmail pictures."

"I told you, they're disgusting."

"Yeah, they're disgusting, but do any of them actually show an aborted fetus or anything else that would prove an abortion was actually performed?"

"Of course an abortion was performed. Gladys would still be pregnant if it wasn't."

"Just answer my question, Jake."

When Doherty still hadn't said anything for several seconds, I gave him a gentle nudge. "What's in the damned pictures, Doherty?"

"They show Gladys on an operating table. Her feet were up in some sort of . . . thing that kept her legs apart. One of the pictures was taken from the head end of the table, another is at an angle from one side, and the last one was shot straight on from the foot end of the table."

"But nothing else?"

"Good god, man! Isn't that enough?"

It wasn't, but I didn't say so. "Alright, Jake. You'll hear from me or Deputy Framm before you get your call from the kidnappers at five."

"What happens if I don't hear from you?"

I said, "You will," and hung up. I just wasn't in the mood for anymore of Jake Doherty and his unhappy little family. Well, at least he didn't tell me to be careful.

Framm was waiting for me outside the phone booth. "Anything new?"

"Nope. I was just keeping my promises to call Samantha Harrison and Jake Doherty by noon. We all set?"

"All except your outfit."

"My outfit?"

"Yeah, most guys don't fish in a sport coat and tie."

"They don't? Guess I'd better take 'em off."

We walked over to the Ford so I could leave my stuff there with Framm's. He watched me transfer the Colt and its spare rounds from my jacket to my pants pocket.

"I figured that's what you had in your jacket. It bulged. If you're gonna carry that thing you ought to get a belt or shoulder holster. Or an ankle rig like I'm wearing."

I gave him a look that said I wasn't interested in adding any such items to my wardrobe and underlined it by saying, "I only take it out for holidays and special occasions."

Framm looked at me the same as he had out on Highway One three days earlier when I'd said some guys never get used to seeing dead bodies. But if he had questions, he kept them to himself again.

I said, "Okay, let's go fishin'."

The boat Framm rented was a sturdy little skiff with an Evenrude air-cooled outboard engine bolted to the transom. Doherty's remarks, along with the anger I already felt over Dandy's kidnapping, made me want to show somebody that I wasn't entirely helpless. So I stepped down onto the skiff's rear seat, gave the Evenrude's mixture knob a twist to the start position and pulled the starter rope.

Fortunately for my ego, the little engine seemed to appreciate such skillful handling and promptly sputtered to life. Up on the dock, Framm was suitably impressed.

"Hey, Atkins! I thought you didn't know anything about boats!"

"I don't know anything about fishing, Will. Boats I know about. Hoist your butt down here and let's get going."

He untied the bow line and stepped down off the dock. I pointed us out into the bay and opened the throttle to the stop. I figured we were somewhere between two and three miles from the inlet on Strawberry Point. The flat-bottomed skiff wasn't built for speed, but the gutsy little engine dug in and pushed us along at something like five or six knots. At that rate, it wouldn't take more than half an hour to reach our destination.

Framm was still curious about my nautical skills. Over the Evenrude's racket, he hollered, "Where the hell did you learn to handle a boat?"

"I was practically raised in Long Beach Harbor. My dad was a tug skipper," I yelled back.

Since conversation was virtually impossible, Framm just nodded and turned around to watch where we were going. I concentrated on my navigation, which wasn't much of a challenge on this trip. We were going straight up the northwest arm of Richardson Bay.

Less than fifteen minutes later, the southern tip of Strawberry Point slid by off to starboard. I moved in a little closer to shore in order to stay out of sight and get the lay of the land. Our warmer June days were beginning to dry out the low rolling hills, leaving them in transition from spring green to summer gold. I also noticed there was no beach along this section of Strawberry's shoreline. The hills came right down to the water, where they abruptly turned to marshes full of reeds and cattails.

After hugging the shore for another ten minutes, I cut the engine. It was suddenly so quiet we could actually hear the cars rumbling along Highway 101 half a mile away. Still, it took a few minutes before the reverberations of the engine left our ears and we stopped shouting at each other.

"Will, the inlet is just around this little point. We'd better start doing whatever it is that fishermen do so we'll look like we belong here."

He turned around on his seat and tied a small lead weight to each of our lines. Framm swung one pole over the port side and let out a little line. He repeated the routine with the other pole on the starboard side.

"If we were really out here for fish, trolling probably wouldn't be the best way to find them, but it gives us an excuse to keep moving. Start up again and follow the shoreline on around very slowly."

I did as Framm said, and several minutes later we putted sedately around the little point and got our first close look at the Davises' house. Actually, we weren't really that close. The inlet was more than a quarter-mile wide and I was tempted to cut directly across it, but that would have made our interest in the house too obvious. That is, if someone were actually there and they had any reason to pay the slightest bit of attention to us.

Gradually moving away from the shore, I eased us a little closer until we'd reached a point not quite halfway across the inlet. I cut the motor again and let the skiff drift.

Framm said, "If we're gonna sit here awhile, pick up your pole. I don't suppose you remembered the binoculars."

I shook my head. "No, damn it. My mind was on those phone calls."

"It's probably just as well. It wouldn't be smart to sit out here staring at them through field glasses."

"Yeah, probably not. Let's hang around out here a little while and watch for some sign of life at the house."

"Okay. Swing your pole out over the transom so you can sit at an angle without facing the place straight on. Hopefully, they won't recognize you from this distance."

"Unless they happen to have a pair of binoculars," I said disgustedly.

Framm grinned. "Don't be so hard on yourself, pal. Relax and have a good time. Remember, this is supposed to be fun. And reel your line in occasionally, and then cast it out again. But don't leave it out of the water long. If anybody is paying attention to us, they might wonder what the hell kind of fish we expect to catch without hooks or bait on our lines."

Letting my eyes wander around the inlet from time to time, as if enjoying our peaceful surroundings, I studied the house. It was an old two-story wood-frame structure with a porch across its northeast side, to our right.

There were also two smaller outbuildings on the property, one on each side of the house. The one nearest the porch was big enough to be a garage. The other was smaller, like a storage shed.

Just past the shed on the southwest side of the house were the eucalyptus trees that shielded the house from the highway. A short distance beyond them was a small stream bed that emptied into the inlet. Another eighth of a mile past the stream, Highway 101 crossed the tip of the little peninsula on low pilings.

A movement caught my eye. I glanced over again and watched a large black sedan wind its way along the road that ran down the hill behind the house.

"Will, you see that?"

"Yeah, is it a Buick?"

"Yup. Look at the front curve of the radiator and the chrome along the hood."

The big car disappeared behind the house for a moment, and when it showed up again I got a glimpse of the right front fender. If it wasn't just wishful thinking, there was a long scrape mark in the sheet metal.

"I think we've got 'em, Will. I'm pretty sure I saw the spot on the right front fender that got banged up when the guy came after me Monday night."

The sedan pulled up short of the larger outbuilding and both front doors opened. They were in the shade of a large oak tree, and about all I could make out were the relative sizes of the two men who stepped down from the running boards. The driver was a big man wearing a fedora and standing nearly a head taller than his passenger. A moment later they disappeared into the house.

"The big guy look familiar, Park?"

"I don't know, Will. I've never actually seen Elaine's killer outside of an automobile. The hat looked right, though. I think it's time we moved on."

Framm nodded, and I started the Evenrude, swinging us around toward the mouth of the inlet. As soon as we'd passed under the highway bridge and could no longer be seen from the house, I cut the motor and pointed our bow into the cattails. The skiff's momentum carried us up against the shore.

Speaking loud enough to be heard over the highway traffic rumbling by a few feet above our heads, Framm asked, "What's the plan, Park?"

Thinking my feeble idea hardly qualified as a plan, I said, "I'm going to get a closer look at that house. We need to find out if Dandy and Gladys are really there. We need to know for sure."

"But how are we going to get close enough to find out?"

"I think I can get over to those eucalyptus trees without being spotted. I might be able to see something from there."

"Okay. What am I supposed to be doing while you're off playing Lone Ranger?"

"If the girls are there, that house is too well situated for us to make any kind of a move without being seen and creating a standoff situation. We need to get them out in the open."

"How do you figure to accomplish that?"

"Davis is going to call Doherty at five, and he has to have the girls with him so he can prove to Jake that they're still alive."

"So?"

"So, what if he couldn't use the phone in the house?"

Framm was beginning to get the picture. "They'd have to go somewhere else to make the call."

"Right. And, this being a fairly rural area, I suspect the telephone service goes out from time to time, so Davis probably wouldn't be too suspicious if he picked up the phone and found it dead."

"But how do we know it's going to be dead when he picks it up?"

"There's a single line of poles leading up to the house. The top wire is the electric service--you can tell by the insulators. The lower one is the telephone. Cut it and the phone goes dead."

"And you expect me to climb a pole and cut the wire?"

"Yeah. If we're right about the girls being there, it will force Davis out into the open with them."

"Okay. How do we work it?"

"I think the best way is for you to take the skiff back and drive my car around to the road that leads out here from Tiburon Boulevard. There's a pair of bolt cutters in the trunk—in the tool box. Remember, cut the bottom wire. Otherwise, you're gonna get a hell of a shock."

Framm was starting to look a little dubious about my brilliant plan. "Then what?"

"Then find a place where you can get out of sight and watch the road. I'll work my way around that hill behind the house and meet you. We'll find a spot where we can set up some kind of a roadblock and stop them on their way to call Doherty."

He didn't look convinced. "It might work. When would we meet up?"

I looked at my watch. "Let's say two hours. It's one-thirty now. I'll try to work my way around to the road by three-thirty."

"What if they discover the phone's out too soon and leave before we meet up?"

"Then it's up to you. Follow them and use your judgment. My guess is they might head for the sanitarium. If the phones are still hooked up there, it's a place where they could take the girls and make their call without attracting a lot of attention. But that's only if the phones are working there."

"I don't know, Park. This is risky as hell. There are too many ways things could go wrong."

"I know. If you've got a better idea, let's hear it."

"We need more help to pull this thing off. At least one man to cover the possibility that they might get out before you and I meet up. They'd be sure to spot me if I tried to follow them too closely on the road out here. And if I hung back and lost them, we could be worse off than we are now, assuming the girls are actually here."

He was right. Having someone to watch Tiburon Boulevard in case something went wrong would eliminate some of the risk, but we didn't have another man. However, I realized, we did have another pair of eyes available.

"Will, I think I know how to improve the odds a little. When you get back to the dock, call KDG and ask for Charlene Blanchard. She's my assistant in the news department. Give Charlie instructions on how to get to Tiburon Boulevard and tell her to find a concealed spot where she can watch the road to Strawberry point. If a black Buick sedan comes out of here, she's to follow at a safe distance. When it stops somewhere, she can call the station and leave a message for me or you, saying where the car went."

"A woman, Park?"

"Hell, she's got as much on the ball as either of us. Probably more."

Framm nodded reluctantly. "Okay, having her watch the road out of here will help. I'll warn her about getting too close if the Buick shows up."

"Good. Here are my car keys. Let's get this show on the road."

Nineteen

The midday traffic on Highway 101 was sporadic. In between the cars and trucks rumbling over the highway bridge, I heard a Meadowlark singing its heart out somewhere in the field that separated me from my objective.

The eucalyptus grove was only an eighth of a mile away—just a little more than the combined lengths of two football fields. It wasn't a long hike by any means, unless you didn't want to be seen.

The ground was flat and offered no cover except for abundant crops of mustard and knee-high needle grass. There was no way to cross it—even on my stomach—without being clearly visible through the trees from the upstairs windows on my side of the house.

The hill behind the house offered the best solution. I could put it between me and those windows by working my way north among the highway pilings. From there I would be out of sight until I reached the creek running down this side of the eucalyptus grove. Hopefully the creek bed would be deep enough to provide some cover until I was opposite the house and cut over into the trees. It was the long way around—in effect, three sides of a rectangle—but it was the only safe choice I had.

When I reached it half an hour later, the creek turned out to be ideal for my purposes. While nearly dry in June, it apparently carried a fair amount of runoff during the winter. The steady flow of all that water had eroded a three-to-four-foot deep course in the soft earth. Dropping into a crouch, I moved quickly along the creek bed to the eucalyptus grove. There I scrambled up the bank and sprinted to the trees' protective shelter.

The shed we'd seen from the skiff was only ten or twelve feet from where I stood. The rear of the main house was just beyond it, no more than twenty feet away. A couple of sagging plank steps between rickety two-by-four handrails led up to a screened back door that was roughly centered in the rear wall of the house. There were two windows on the ground floor, one on each side of the door halfway between the door and the corner of the house. The second floor had three windows set in the weathered wooden siding, one above each of the first floor windows and a narrower opening above the back door.

The shade on the ground floor window closest to me was pulled down tight, but the window to my right, on the other side of the back door, appeared to be open. Hoping to get a look inside, I began working my way in that direction.

I'd taken no more than three steps when a raucous squeak from the screened door stopped me in my tracks. I stood stock still between two gray, peeling eucalyptus trunks and waited for the guy who was coming down the steps to look up and see my white shirt, brilliant as a neon sign in the shady grove.

But Doctor Donald Davis was a man on a mission. He headed straight for the shed without so much as a glance in my direction. I assumed it was Davis because he fit Ed Tompkin's sketchy description of the man who'd waited in the car while Mary Davis came in to buy peppermint schnapps.

He was slender and about my height—around five-ten. His hair was sandy brown and I placed him somewhere in his thirties, though that could have been way off because he had one of those soft, lineless faces that never age. Davis wore dark gray slacks with maroon suspenders and a white shirt open at the collar. He rolled his sleeves up in a very business-like manner as he walked.

Davis stopped in front of the shed, fished around in his pocket, and came up with a ring of keys. He used one of them to open a padlock that secured the shed door and disappeared inside.

It was one of those opportunities that seem too good to pass up, even if it meant tossing a plan out the window. I moved toward the shed as quietly as I could through the dry leaves and spears of eucalyptus bark.

At the edge of the grove I was close enough to make out Davis' form inside the dark interior of the shed. His back was to me and he was leaning over, fiddling with an electric motor. The shed seemed to be a pump house. I guessed they were having trouble with the pump, and Davis had come out to fix it.

I was ten feet from the door. If he didn't turn around and nobody else came out of the house, I had him. Colt in hand, I covered the remaining distance and stepped through the pump house door.

"Don't move a muscle, Davis."

Startled, he began a reflex turn in my direction, saw the Colt, and froze. I moved left, out of the doorway and further into the shadowy confines of the eight-by-ten shed. His eyes followed the barrel of my thirty-eight.

"On your knees. Put your hands together and stretch them out over that pipe."

Davis followed my instructions to the letter, dropping to his knees and resting his arms on the sturdy-looking piece of pump plumbing I'd indicated. I glanced around the shed and found what I needed hanging on a nail to my right. It was a length of insulated wire, probably left over from the pump installation.

I grabbed the wire and said in a low voice, "Davis, I firmly believe the world would be a much better place if I blew you straight to hell. All it'll take is one false move."

Davis didn't make any moves, false or otherwise. He just watched as, holding on to one end, I dropped the coil of wire to the ground. I put a foot on the coil so I could pull against it and tied his wrists to the pipe with the other end.

When he was secure, I pocketed the Colt and stuffed the greasiest rag I could find into his mouth. I found some black cloth friction tape with just enough left on the roll to wrap around Davis' head twice, holding the gag in place.

Gagging Davis almost seemed unnecessary because he hadn't made a sound since I walked into the shed. I'd figured him for an amateur, but I was beginning to have some doubts. The man was either scared out of his wits or one cool customer. It bothered me that I couldn't tell which.

Checking his pockets, I found nothing more deadly than keys, a three inch pocketknife and his wallet, which contained a fair-sized stack of twenties and a California drivers' license identifying him as Donald M. Davis, M. D. I stuffed the wallet back into his pocket, put the keys in my pocket and used the knife to cut an eight foot length from the other end of the wire that held Davis' wrists.

Looping one end of the wire around his neck, I tied Davis' ankles with the other end, leaving the good doctor trussed up like a hog-tied calf. I double-checked my knots to be sure they wouldn't slip and dropped his knife into my shirt pocket.

Feeling reasonably certain Davis wasn't going anywhere, I peeked out the door to make sure the coast was still clear. It was, but I couldn't count on it staying that way much longer. Davis had come out here to fix something. Since he hadn't changed into work clothes, I figured the repair wasn't major and he'd be expected back in the house soon.

If I was going to pull this off, I needed to move quickly. Assuming the men we'd seen arriving in the Buick were Elaine's killer and Davis, it was a pretty safe bet that Dandy and Gladys were here, too. And Davis' wife would be in the house as well. She was probably watching the girls while the men were out.

So if I could get the drop on Mary and the guy with the big jaw, I was home free. But that was bound to be harder than it sounded. Everything depended on where they were in the house.

Davis moved, shifting his weight a little. I glanced down and he was still staring at me with the same blank, almost calm, expression on his face. Was it resignation? Or did he know something I didn't?

I stepped out into the bright sunshine again and snapped the padlock into its hasp, locking the pump house door. At the back steps, I remembered the squeaky screened door. Inside, they would surely hear the racket, but they might think I was Davis coming back. At least, I hoped that's what they would think. Either way, I wouldn't have much time to reconnoiter the house.

From the steps I could see that the wooden door beyond the screen was open. So with the Colt firmly in my right hand again, I opened the screeching screened door and stepped inside.

It was a typical mid-western farmhouse; similar to one I remember visiting as a kid on a trip to Ohio with my folks. I was in a long narrow central hallway that ran the entire length of the house, ending at the front door. Since anyone who came into the hall would see me standing there silhouetted against the open back door, I kept moving.

The first door on my left was closed, but the one to my right stood open. It led to the kitchen, and the hardwood floorboards creaked a little as I stepped through it, but there was no one in the kitchen to hear them.

By modern residential standards it was a huge room with a high ceiling and plenty of space to prepare meals for a hungry farm family. A narrow archway in the wall to my left led to another, shorter hall that ended in a room at the front of the house. Judging by what I could see of a table and some chairs, it was the dining room. I walked in that direction.

" . . . a ten-letter word that means in love with one's self?"

It was a woman's voice. I stopped and listened as a low male voice grumbled a short, negative-sounding reply. The woman said something back about a big dumb palooka, and I concluded that they were still some distance away, in another part of the house.

I looked cautiously into the dining room and saw another archway that opened back onto the central hall. Across the hall, I could see most of the front room. Nobody home there, either.

Moving across the dining room, I looked back up the central hall. It widened out and opened onto something like a parlor behind the living room, but my view was too narrow to see beyond the arched entrance.

Now the male voice was much clearer. "What the hell is taking your husband so long out there?"

"Oh, that darn pump is always giving us fits, Ike. He'll be back in a few minutes."

They were in the parlor, and behind their voices I could make out the only possible reason for them thinking Davis was still outside. They didn't hear the screened door because the radio was on. The announcer informed his audience that they were enjoying Meredith Wilson's orchestra on KGO.

Sensing that my time was growing short, I stepped out of the dining room and across the hall. A few feet further down, the parlor entrance was directly opposite another, narrower archway. Through it, I could see a set of stairs that went up three steps to a small landing, turned right, and climbed out of sight behind the hallway wall.

"Well, I'm gonna go see what's takin' him so long."

That was my entrance cue. I stepped into the parlor and said, "You aren't going anywhere, Ike."

As expected, Ike turned out to be the fellow with the comic strip jaw. He was facing me about six feet away when I stepped into view, and his first instinct was to reach for the revolver in his shoulder holster. But his arm stopped about belt-high when he saw that my Colt was pointed directly at his chest. Ike knew damned well I wasn't likely to miss at that range.

"What the hell are you doin' here?"

It was one of those stupid things tough guys say when they get caught with their pants down. It didn't deserve an answer, and he didn't expect one. Instead, I said, "Just stay right where you are. Raise your hands and put them behind your head."

The woman was sitting at a small table under the window at the far end of the room. Ed Tompkin had been right. Mary Davis was very pretty. I knew it was her because she had green eyes, reddish-brown curly hair, and a beauty mark above her upper lip. The only thing that was missing from Tompkin's description was the friendly smile.

Missus Davis wasn't smiling any kind of smile. She just looked surprised, her eyes wide open and moving quickly back and forth between Ike and me. She expected him to do something, but the big man was just bright enough to see that the odds were stacked against him. I don't think he even considered taking advantage of the brief opportunity I gave him when I stepped close enough to pull the revolver from his shoulder holster.

I stuck his pistol into my belt and said, "Back up to that chair and sit down."

While Ike was backing into the chair, I glanced at Mary Davis again. She was looking in my direction, but it took me a fraction of a second too long to realize she wasn't looking at me. Her eyes were focused on something behind me.

Alec handled it very well. He must have come down the stairs behind me, then across the hall without a sound. Mary Davis had given me just enough warning to catch Doherty's houseman out of the corner of my eye . . . right before he clubbed me.

As Dashiell Hammet might have put it, a brilliant burst of white hot pain exploded in my skull. Then the lights went out and I felt myself being sucked down into an endless whirlpool that dragged me deeper and deeper into its blackness. Hammet ought to try it sometime. The experience isn't nearly as thrilling as it sounds.

Twenty

There were formulae all over the blackboard. My high school algebra teacher, Missus Gilliam, kept pointing at them with her yardstick and asking for the value of X. But no matter how I tried, the answer wouldn't come out right. There was something missing from the equation—another unknown quantity.

Missus Gilliam shook her head in disappointment and said, "Parker . . . Parker . . . Parker!"

I studied the symbols on the board until my brain ached, and I still couldn't figure in out.

"Parker . . . Parker . . . ."

How did Missus Gilliam expect me to think when she kept shaking my shoulders and repeating my name? Especially with my head pounding like it was.

"Parker!"

I mumbled something like, "I can't figure it out."

Then Missus Gilliam said my name again in a voice that didn't sound like hers anymore. Now she sounded like Dandy.

"Parker, wake up!"

I forced my eyes open. It was Dandy. But the sunlight coming in the windows made my head throb even worse, so I closed my eyes and wondered what Dandy was doing in my high school algebra class.

"Parker, please! Wake up!"

She made it sound important, so I tried opening my eyes again. I discovered we weren't in Missus Gilliam's classroom, we were in a bedroom. I could tell because I was on a bed.

"Is he alright?"

There was someone else in the room with us. I thought about that for a moment and decided it sounded like Gladys Doherty.

Suddenly my world started sliding back into focus and making sense again.

I was on my back, and the ceiling floating over my head seemed very far away. That was a clue that probably meant I was still in the old house on Strawberry Point.

I slowly lowered my gaze and braved a look into the glare outside the window beyond the end of the bed. It hurt my eyes and made me squint. All I could make out was a brilliant blue sky above some vague grayish-green foliage that might have been the tops of eucalyptus trees. Another clue. From it, I deduced that I was in a second floor room, facing the highway.

Feeling quite pleased with myself, I expanded my quest for knowledge by glancing to the left. That's where Dandy was. She was sitting on the bed. When I looked at her, she leaned over, touched my forehead, and said, "How do you feel, Darling?"

I wanted a better look at Dandy, so I turned my head toward her. That was a mistake. I rolled onto the spot where Alec hit me and a burst of pain made the lights start flashing off and on again.

I winced and groaned an answer to Dandy's question. "Like something the cat dragged in."

"You've got an awful lump on your head. I was afraid you had a concussion or something."

From the way the room and Dandy's face kept blurring, it seemed wise not to rule that possibility out quite yet. When I finally managed to keep Dandy in focus for a few seconds, I noticed the large bruise covering most of her left cheek. It was swollen and mostly yellow with some red and black mixed in.

Even with all the discoloration and swelling on her face, Dandy was still the prettiest sight I'd seen in quite a while. But the bruise made me angry, and I wanted to know how it got there.

Thickly, I asked, "Who hit you, Dandy?"

She touched the spot on her face. "You mean this? It was Alec. I don't think he likes me very much and he certainly doesn't think much of you. He hit me with his fist and said it was a down payment on what he owed my boyfriend. And while we're on the subject, what happened to your face?"

It took me a moment to realize she was talking about the bandages. They'd been there so long I'd gotten used to them.

"Ike took a couple of shots at me Monday night. This was the result of a close miss. No serious damage done."

Dandy looked shocked. "He tried to kill you? Why?"

My vision was improving. For the first time, I could see Gladys standing a few feet behind Dandy. My reasoning ability was improving as well. I remembered the formulae on Missus Gilliam's blackboard and understood what my subconscious was trying to tell me.

From the very beginning, there'd been pieces of this puzzle that didn't fit quite right. They disturbed me because I couldn't come up with a single scenario that would work for all of them. But now that Alec had suddenly shown up where he had no business being, there was an explanation that made all the pieces fall neatly into place. Gladys Doherty had to be the unknown quantity in the equation.

I looked back at Dandy and said, "Ike tried to kill me because he knew I could identify him as Elaine's killer." I paused, did my best to look Gladys straight in the eye, and added, "But there's a lot more to it, isn't there, Gladys?"

Dandy frowned and stared at me for a second before she turned to look at her friend. Gladys was busy looking innocent as hell, but she wasn't very good at it. Even with my unsteady vision, I'd seen the flicker of apprehension in her eyes and knew for sure I'd found the unknown quantity.

In a tone that wasn't very convincing, Gladys said, "Parker, I don't know what you mean."

"Oh come on, Gladys. Give up the act. You've been in this scheme up to your neck right from the start."

Dandy wasn't understanding any of it. "Parker, what's gotten into you?"

With an effort that made the exploits of Jack Armstrong pale by comparison, I sat up and swung my legs over the edge of the bed. The movement set off a new round of pounding in my skull and a wave of nausea that almost got the better of me.

When the room stopped spinning again, I said, "Dandy, your pal Gladys and the good doctor downstairs staged a phony pregnancy and a bogus abortion to set her grandfather up for blackmail."

Gladys was still protesting her innocence. "No! I was pregnant! They took pictures . . . ."

"Oh, they took pictures, alright. And you had to know they were taking them. It must have been embarrassing as hell, but that's what made the scheme work. Jacob was so shocked he never suspected that his loving granddaughter would willingly pose for such indecent photos. The problem is the pictures don't really show anything that proves an abortion actually took place. As long as the blackmailers had gone that far, there was only one reason not to include the aborted fetus in the pictures . . . because there was none to photograph."

Gladys turned away and Dandy said, "Parker, you've got to be wrong. I don't know anything about the pictures you're talking about, but why would Gladys blackmail her own family?"

"You'll have to ask her about that. Or you might ask Alec. He was in on the deal, too. Gladys recruited Alec as a middle man to arrange the bogus abortion so there'd be no direct contact between her and Davis. Jacob Doherty would have wondered how his debutante granddaughter knew where to get an abortion, but it was the sort of thing a guy like Alec might know or could find out."

Dandy turned to look at Gladys. The big blonde was standing at the window with her back to us. When Dandy looked at me again, she was frowning.

"Parker, they killed Elaine! Are you saying Gladys helped murder her own sister?"

Gladys spun around before I could answer and cried, "No! I never would have hurt Elaine! I didn't know . . . ."

She sank into a wooden chair next to the window, sobbing uncontrollably. Dandy went to Gladys and touched her shoulders lightly while looking at me for some kind of explanation.

"I doubt if she knew anything about that, Dandy. In fact, I don't think Gladys even made the connection between her scheme with Davis and Elaine's death until Monday afternoon when I finally convinced her that Elaine had been murdered. Then she was forced to put two and two together and accept the fact that Davis or Ike killed her sister."

In a quiet voice that was punctuated with sobs, Gladys said, "Elaine found the pictures . . . she . . . I had to tell her . . . tell her I was being blackmailed. I made her promise . . . Elaine promised she wouldn't get . . . involved. But she called the sanitarium anyway. Donald was there. She told him he had to meet her . . . at that dance place in Larkspur and . . . and hand over the picture negatives or . . . or she would tell the police about him doing abor . . . . abortions. That's . . . that's why they killed her. Elaine was only . . . trying to help me."

"And," I said, "When you realized Davis was responsible for Elaine's death, you called him, too. You told him the deal was off, didn't you?"

Gladys looked up at us. Both cheeks were glistening with tears, but there was fury in her eyes now. "I told him he was a monster! I . . . I told him I was going to tell the police who killed . . . . who killed Elaine."

"But Davis warned you not to do that because he would implicate you in the blackmail scheme and the cops would think you were in on Elaine's murder."

She nodded and buried her face in her hands. Dandy looked down at her friend. There wasn't much sympathy in her eyes. After watching Gladys for a moment, Dandy looked at me and said, "Is all this . . . this kidnapping business phony, too?"

"No," I said. "I'm afraid it's the real McCoy. I doubt if Davis ever intended for Ike to kill Elaine. But he did and suddenly they were facing charges of murder in the first degree. My guess is Davis figured to beat the murder wrap by eliminating the only two witnesses against them. With Gladys and me out of the picture, the case was mostly circumstantial. It probably wouldn't even have gone to trial.

"I must have been the greatest threat, so Davis sent Ike after me first. But Ike missed and I led the cops to the murder vehicle, which has already been traced to Davis. So I think they figured the only option left was to take it on the lam, and Davis came up with this kidnapping scheme to kill two birds with one stone. They eliminate a witness, Gladys, and pick up some quick traveling money. They can go a long way on a hundred g's."

There was a look of realization in Dandy's eyes. "Then they have to kill all of us, don't they?"

"I'm afraid that's the way Davis sees it. The Lindbergh Law made kidnapping a federal capital offense. He has to be figuring they're in so deep already that another murder or two won't make much difference one way or the other. I'm sure he intended to kill Gladys all along. Now, thanks to my bumbling, they get me as a bonus. The sad part is that you got roped into this just because you were in the wrong place at the wrong time."

If I'd thought about it, I could have predicted Dandy's response to the situation. It was typical of the way she looked at things.

Dandy simply said, "Then we have to find a way out of here, don't we?"

I nodded and looked at my watch. It was quarter to four. If Framm was on schedule, he'd already cut the telephone line and was waiting for me to show up. What would he do when I didn't?

More to the point, what was I going to do? The answer to that depended on my physical limitations. My head was still pounding like crazy, but my vision was better and I seemed to be thinking more or less rationally.

It was time to try something really strenuous, like standing up. I did it slowly because I wasn't sure my head wouldn't fall off and roll around on the floor if I moved too quickly.

As I straightened, a little wave of nausea hit me and I wobbled. Dandy was immediately at my side.

"Parker, be careful. What do you think you're doing?"

In a whisper, I said, "Just what you said . . . trying to find a way out of here. Take a look through the keyhole and see if anybody's out in the hall."

While Dandy went to the door, I steered a zigzag course to the window. I was examining the ten penny nails they'd driven through the window frame to secure it when she came back.

Dandy whispered, "The one with the big jaw—Ike, I guess—is sitting out there in the hall. He's probably heard every word we said."

Thinking back on our conversation, I decided no serious beans had been spilled. From that point on, however, we'd have to be a little more careful. The problem was there wasn't much to be careful about. I had no idea how to get how to get away from Davis. The only constructive thing I could think of was to tell Dandy and Gladys about the plan I'd concocted with Framm and hope one of us came up with some way to salvage what was left of it.

I looked at Gladys and knew I couldn't expect much help from her. She was just sitting there, staring off into space. I had to say her name twice before she surfaced from her trance and looked at me.

"Gladys," I whispered, "Slide your chair over here next to the bed so we can talk about how to get out of here."

She looked at me blankly for a moment before standing up and moving her chair. I sat on the end of the bed and Dandy plunked down next to me.

Keeping my voice low, I said, "A San Mateo County Sheriff's Deputy came up here with me. We found this house and guessed it might be where Davis was holding you. If we were right, it would be impossible to get you out safely because the place is too well protected. So we came up with a plan that would force Davis to take you out of here himself.

"He's supposed to call Jake at five with the ransom instructions. Our idea was for Framm—the deputy—to cut the telephone wires to this place, forcing Davis to make his call from somewhere else. He has to take you two with him because Jake told him there wouldn't be any payoff unless Davis could prove both of you were still alive.

"My job was to make sure you were here, then meet Framm to set up a roadblock of some kind where we could stop Davis' car out in the open. Of course, I won't be there now, so I don't know if Framm will go ahead on his own or not."

Gladys was staring off into space again, but Dandy was paying rapt attention. She whispered, "What if he doesn't?"

"That depends on how Davis sets up the payoff. Since he doesn't plan to turn you loose, my guess is he'll bring you back here before he goes for the ransom money. That would be safer than driving around with you in the car."

Dandy nodded and asked the next logical question. "Will Davis take you along with us when he goes to call Jacob?"

"I wouldn't if I were him. There's no reason to. It would be safer to leave me behind with Ike or Alec."

I didn't mention the other likelihood, which was that they would probably pick that time to kill me. I imagined Ike or Alec coming in the bedroom to blow my brains out and an idea occurred to me. If whoever came in thought I was still unconscious, they might be a little less careful.

I told Dandy about the thought, explaining it as a way to insure that Davis didn't take me along so that I'd have a chance to even the odds a little before they got back from calling Doherty. She spotted the flaw in my plan right away.

"Park, if Ike's been out there all this time, he's heard your voice and knows you're awake."

"Then I'll just have to pass out again. But before I do that, I need to find a weapon of some kind."

Dandy glanced around the room and said, "That will be difficult. There isn't much in here."

She was right. Besides the bed, the room contained the chair Gladys was sitting on and an overhead light fixture. That was it. Of course, I'd already checked the pockets in my slacks. They'd taken the Colt, along with everything else.

I might pry a leg off the chair, but that would be noticed the minute anyone came in. I considered the bed and wondered if there might be something under it.

Slipping onto my knees, I bent over to look. Instantly the room began spinning so violently I almost missed the fact that something fell out of my shirt pocket. When the dizziness passed, I looked down to see what had dropped out of my pocket.

It was the knife I'd taken from Davis in the pump house. They'd missed it in my shirt pocket. It was too small to be an effective weapon, but it was a start.

Moving more slowly this time, I bent down again and looked under the bed. Aside from a few cobwebs, I found nothing. The bed frame itself was a simple affair made out of redwood two-by-fours with some slats between them to support the mattress.

Preparing to stand up again, I slid my hand along the frame end-rail and promptly picked up a large splinter from its rough surface. I pulled the needle-sharp piece of redwood out of my palm and looked at the offending board. The reason I'd gotten the splinter was immediately apparent. The wood had dried, and a long crack had split open. I tested the cracked piece and discovered that if I pried carefully on the end that had given me the splinter, it would break off a fourteen or fifteen inch-long section that tapered from a width of about two inches to a sharp point, something like a dagger.

I opened Davis' knife and used the blade as a wedge to help separate the piece I wanted from the bed frame. It snapped off right where I hoped it would.

Dandy leaned over to see what I was doing and said quietly, "Is that what you're going to use as . . . ."

"Yeah. With a little trimming, it should work just fine."

I sat on the bed with my back to the keyhole in the door. After relaxing for a second to let the pounding in my head subside, I began sharpening the point and edges of my makeshift dagger with Davis' knife. I also smoothed and notched the hilt end for a better grip. When my handiwork was done, I swept the shavings under the bed, slipped the little pocketknife back into my pocket, and thought about how to stage my lapse back into unconsciousness.

The plan I came up with was simple, and our performance was quite realistic—almost too realistic. I took a couple of staggering steps and collapsed to the floor, nearly passing out for real from the jarring impact.

Dandy knelt at my side, and after failing to revive me, she recruited Gladys' help to lift me onto a prearranged spot on the bed. Once there, I reached under a fold in the quilt with my right hand and grasped the wooden dagger. Finally, Dandy sat on the bed between my head and the door so we could whisper back and forth without being seen from the keyhole.

I had no idea if my thumping to the floor, along with Dandy's and Gladys' concerned dialogue, was wasted on Ike or not. I hoped he was paying attention simply because I hated to think we'd gone through all that for nothing.

I asked Dandy to look at my watch. She said it was four-thirty-five. Whatever was going to happen would happen in the next twenty-five minutes.

Twenty One

The first indication I had that they were coming was some muffled conversation out in the hall. Mary Davis was talking to Ike. I heard her say, " . . . call the old man . . . ." and something about unlocking the door.

Feigning unconsciousness with my eyes closed, I couldn't see what was going on. But what I heard gave me the impression that Ike wasn't taking any chances.

A key turned in the lock with a distinct click and the door flew open with such force that it banged against the wall behind it. There was a moment of silence followed by Ike's voice.

"What's his story?"

Dandy sounded truly concerned. "He passed out again, and I can't wake him up. You have to get him a doctor."

I almost winced. Dandy had forgotten that there was, in fact, already a doctor in the house. The last thing we needed was Davis coming up here and discovering that I was faking. Fortunately, Mary Davis wasn't very concerned about my health.

She said, "Don can come up and look at him later. Right now we need you downstairs. Both of you. Come out here into the hall."

I heard Dandy and Gladys walking across the hardwood floor and out into the hall. Someone slammed the door and locked it. After that, I heard their footsteps fading into the distance. A few minutes later, there were more footsteps out in the hall. When the door didn't open, I assumed it was Ike, or maybe Alec, coming up to keep an eye on me while the phone call was made downstairs.

From my point of view, nothing else happened for quite a while and I began to wonder if Framm ever cut the wire. Then I knew he had. This time the voices out in the hall were both male.

Since I didn't recognize the first voice and the only one of the four I hadn't actually heard speak was Davis, it had to be him. He was loud and angry.

"The damned telephone is out again! We'll have to take the women up to the sanitarium and call old man Doherty from there."

A deep bass voice I remembered from Jake Doherty's warehouse on pier forty-two rumbled a question in reply, something about going along to the sanitarium. Davis' reply was quieter then, and I only caught a few words.

"No . . . three of us . . . handle that . . . I've got another . . . one you'll really enjoy."

I heard Alec's response very clearly. "So you want me to kill that son of a bitch in there?"

"Yes. And . . . out in the bay . . . found. Wait until . . . ."

Alec said a word or two I couldn't make out, and Davis left, the sound of his footsteps leaving me with the impression of someone in a hurry. I adjusted my grip on the redwood dagger and waited.

It wasn't until after I heard the Buick start up and drive away that Alec unlocked the door. I thought he might have looked through the keyhole first to see if I was still on the bed because when Alec came in, he wasn't nearly as cautious as Ike had been.

Alec simply opened the door and walked in. He stopped somewhere between the door and the bed, apparently watching me. A moment later I heard the distinctive click of a revolver being cocked. It sounded like the crack of doom in that quiet room, and for a few frightening seconds I thought Alec might shoot me right then and there, without ever coming close enough for me to use my weapon.

I was just about to take a rolling dive off the opposite side of the bed when Alec said, "Alright, you son of a bitch, cut the act. I know you're fakin'."

I didn't move a muscle, and he took a couple of steps toward the end of the bed. After another tense pause, he said, "Come on, Atkins. Wake up. I want you to know who's about to blow your damn brains out."

When I still didn't move, Alec continued around the foot of the bed. That was exactly where I wanted him to go. I was on my left side at the edge of the bed farthest from the door. To reach me without leaning clear across the bed, Alec had to come all the way around to the side opposite the door. My right hand, gripping the dagger, was in front of me, concealed by the quilt. In order for me to do any serious damage, he had to be behind me and close.

Suddenly, I felt the hard barrel of his pistol between my shoulder blades. It was time.

Alec had transferred the pistol to his left hand and was reaching toward me with his right when I rolled hard in his direction, pinning Alec's gun and arm under my back. At the same time, I thrust the dagger in an arc toward where I figured his chest would be. Opening my eyes in mid-roll, I realized my aim was way too high. I tried to make a last second correction and saw his right arm coming up to deflect the dagger. The sharp piece of redwood hit something hard and Alec pulled the trigger.

Searing pain streaked across my back, and I rolled frantically back to my left, scrambling to reach the edge of the bed before he fired again. Braced for the impact of a second slug, I rolled off the bed and hit the floor on my back with more than enough force to make the room go spinning. Too dazed to move, I lay there waiting for the bullet that would end the life of Parker T. Atkins.

After a very long time, I got tired of waiting. The bedroom was deathly quiet. Maybe I was dead already and just didn't know it. No, that wasn't right. If I was dead, I shouldn't be able to feel pain, and I was feeling a lot of it. The bullet wound in my back was throbbing in precise rhythm with the pounding in my head.

Moving gingerly, I began testing my various extremities and concluded that the slug must not have hit anything too vital because everything seemed to work and there was no numbness. Far from it. Everything hurt like hell.

Next question: Why hadn't Alec finished me off? I was curious about that, but not curious enough to try standing up yet. Instead, I rolled carefully toward the bed. The quilt had slid down on my side when I rolled to the floor. I lifted the quilt and looked under the bed.

He was over there on the other side, alright. I could see Alec on the floor and he wasn't moving. Why wasn't he moving?

I thought about that and decided the blood might explain why he wasn't moving. There was a surprisingly large pool of it under the bed, between me and Alec's head. At the time it seemed like he'd deflected my thrust with the wooden dagger. Maybe I hadn't missed after all.

Curiosity about that and about how badly I was wounded finally provided enough motivation for me to try standing up. Using the edge of the bed for support, I slowly got to my feet, and my old pal nausea rushed right up to greet me. I sat on the bed to let it pass and noticed a burned spot on the bed sheet where Alec's pistol had gone off.

There was a hole in the middle of the spot. That was odd. I stuck my finger in the hole and found that it was deep and angled sharply toward the door. Sliding back onto my knees, I pushed the quilt out of the way and lifted the edge of the mattress. There was a corresponding hole in the bottom of it. I looked down at the bed frame and felt a little silly. There, buried in one of the slats, was Alec's spent slug. Obviously, if it was there, it couldn't be in me.

I reached around and tentatively touched the wound on my back. My hand came away with a small smear of blood on it, but not enough to indicate any major damage. My skin was just badly burned from the muzzle blast. The burn stung like hell, but it was hardly fatal.

Feeling considerably better about things, I decided to have a look at Alec. I moved slowly around the end of the bed and saw that I'd been lucky on another count. My makeshift redwood dagger was stuck in Alec's neck just below his Adam's apple to a depth of about four inches. With all that blood, it must have punctured a major artery. For the second time in two days, I felt for Alec's pulse. This time I did not find it.

Alec's revolver, an ancient and slightly rusty-looking large caliber Webley, was on the floor near his feet. I picked the heavy pistol up, cocked its hammer and walked cautiously out into the hall. A few hours earlier I'd made the mistake of assuming I knew who was in the house. Even though it seemed likely that Alec and I were alone, I wasn't about to make the same mistake twice.

There were three more bedrooms and a bathroom on the second floor. I made sure they were all empty before venturing downstairs. The only things of any interest at all in the rest of the house were my wallet, cigarettes and lighter on the small table in the parlor. My Colt was there, too. I stuck Alec's revolver in the waistband of my slacks and pocketed the Colt and its spare rounds, though I hadn't the slightest idea what I was going to do with all that artillery.

I used my old brass trench lighter to get a Camel going and tried to think. It was five-forty. They'd been gone nearly half an hour, and I had no idea what Framm had done, if anything, to stop them. The only idea I could come up with was to hike out and look for Framm.

Fifty feet from the house, the road began its ascending curve around the hill. I hiked steadily for fifteen minutes before I had to stop and let the pounding in my head subside.

I was halfway around the hill on its west side, and off in the distance I could see the evening fog already cascading in over the coastal hills. The top half of Mount Tamalpais was already lost in the white billowing mass. Less than a quarter mile from where I stood, Highway 101 was choked with homeward-bound commuters. Just beyond the highway I thought I could make out the L-shape of Twin Oaks Sanitarium among the deep afternoon shadows. Was Dandy there?

The thought had occurred to me even before Davis took her and Gladys away that I might never see Dandy again. If Davis had gotten past Framm and made his phone call, Dandy and Gladys would be excess baggage now. It wasn't likely that Jake Doherty could have stalled the payoff any longer. Whether Doherty agreed to pay the ransom or not, the girls had outlived their usefulness and there was no reason for Davis to risk taking them back to the house.

Shoving those gloomy thoughts to the back of my mind, I took a deep breath and resumed my trek. After five more minutes of putting one foot in front of the other, I finally rounded the north side of the hill and looked out across the upper half of Strawberry Point.

There was something going on down there. From my vantage point, it looked like a cross-country automobile race. Three dust clouds were moving in my direction. The lead car was a big black sedan. Several hundred yards behind the sedan, I could make out a coupe that appeared to be the same shade of brown as my Ford. Well behind the coupe, another vehicle I couldn't make out at that distance was trying to keep up with the first two.

The sedan wasn't much more than a mile away, so I didn't waste time trying to figure out why Framm was chasing Davis back toward the house. It didn't matter. What mattered was stopping them before they got there.

I half-jogged, half-staggered down the hill to a point just before the road flattened out. Stopping beside a medium-sized boulder that might provide some cover if my idea didn't work, I pulled Alec's big Webley from my waistband.

Still weak-kneed and trying to catch my breath from running down the hill, I watched the Buick come closer. It was no more than a quarter mile from me, and I could clearly hear the roar of its big engine. What did Osgood Bledsoe's brochure say? An in-line eight with one hundred and twenty horsepower? Something like that.

At the Los Angeles Police Academy they teach you to stand sideways to your target with your right arm extended toward it and your left hand supporting your right elbow. I stood smack in the middle of the road, assumed that stance and hoped I looked menacing as hell.

I looked down the Webley's sights and lined them up with the Buick's driver-side windshield. Of course, it was all a bluff. I could see the silhouettes of the driver and more than two passengers, which meant Dandy and Gladys were in the car. If I fired a round through the windshield, there was a good chance of hitting the wrong person. If forced to shoot, about the only thing I could do was fire into the Buick's grille and hope one of the Webley's big slugs hit something vital, though the odds of actually stopping the car were pretty slim. I hoped the driver was too busy to figure all that out.

The Buick closed within a hundred yards and showed no sign of slowing. The only indication that they even noticed me was the pistol that suddenly appeared out of a passenger-side window. A small geyser of dust spouted up from the dirt road about twenty feet in front of me.

While one part of my mind was busy calculating how much longer I could stand there looking menacing before the Buick flattened me or whoever was shooting got lucky, another part of my mind was amazed at how calmly I was taking all of this. Maybe Alec short-circuited my judgment when he thunked me on the head.

Ike's next shot—they were close enough that I could see Davis behind the wheel—threw up another puff of dirt less than five feet away. The calculating part of my mind screamed, "Now!"

Lowering the Webley a notch, I pointed it in the general direction of the Buick's rapidly approaching grille and squeezed the trigger twice in quick succession. Then Davis slammed on the brakes, and I dove toward the boulder on my right.

I caught a glimpse of the Buick's rear end coming around in my direction as its brakes locked up and the tires lost traction on the dirt road. I landed hard a few feet short of the boulder and thought for a second that the impact of hitting the ground had done me in once and for all. The world went hazy again, and I got the impression of a big chrome thing coming at me. It was the Buick's massive rear bumper, and some part of my brain that was still functioning strongly suggested I do something about the situation.

Scooting around to get my legs out of the way, I scrambled backwards and careened off the boulder. I landed face down in the weeds as the Buick's rear tires skidded past, spraying me with dirt and gravel. The bumper slid over my head with only inches to spare.

Through the mist in my brain and the dust cloud churned up by skidding tires, I watched the sedan spin almost completely around and jerk to a stop twenty or thirty feet further up the road. Davis must have finally gotten his foot off the brake pedal, because the Buick started rolling slowly back down the hill until its front tires bumped into the berm along the far side of the road.

The dust began to settle and a mechanical whining sound came from the motionless Buick. After several seconds, my sluggish brain finally recognized it as the starter. The big engine had died during the skid, and Davis was trying to get it going again.

Another sound groped its way through the fog in my head. It was coming from the other side of the boulder, and I guessed Framm had arrived in my Ford.

Ike confirmed this by throwing open the rear passenger-side door and scrambling out. He reached back into the car and dragged Dandy after him. She landed on her knees, and in a single motion Ike stooped, wrapped his left arm around her waist and hoisted Dandy back onto her feet.

From the other side of the boulder Framm yelled, "Police! Freeze!"

I thought the deputy sounded very convincing, but Ike wasn't impressed. He raised the revolver in his right hand and jerked off a round in Framm's direction. The slug pinged off of something metal, and Ike jabbed the hot gun barrel into Dandy's neck.

She winced, and he yelled, "Drop your gun or the broad gets it here and now!"

The fact that Ike wasn't treating the woman I loved in a very gentlemanly manner finally forced my single-track brain to think about something besides the nasty chip his slug must have taken out of my paint job.

Ike yelled at Framm again with an intensity in his voice that scared the hell out of me. "Drop the damn gun now! Or I swear I'll blow her brains out!"

It was more the sound of Ike's voice than his words that dragged me up out of my stupor. He was desperate, maybe even a little scared, and I didn't doubt for a moment that Ike would kill Dandy without hesitation, even if it meant he'd die in the process.

As the fog gradually cleared from my brain, I started getting the idea that I should do something about all this, and I was trying to think what that something might be when I noticed that Donald and Mary Davis weren't in the Buick anymore. Before, I'd been able to see them through the windshield. Now they were gone.

They must have gotten out the driver's door. I couldn't say for sure because part of my view was blocked by a robust mustard plant in the weed patch where I'd landed after dodging the Buick. One of the things I could see, however, was Alec's Webley. It was in the road about ten feet away, exactly where I'd dropped it.

Seeing the Webley reminded me of the Colt in my pocket, but reaching for it didn't seem like a very good idea. Ike's attention was focused on Framm, but I was well within his line of sight. The only reason for Ike ignoring me had to be that he figured me for unconscious or dead. If I tried to get at the Colt, he'd see the movement and have plenty of time to do something about it, like shoot me.

Ike repeated his demand to Framm for what I what I was pretty sure would be the last time. "You've got three seconds to drop the gun or I'll splatter her brains all over the place. One . . . two . . . ."

Framm must have figured it the same way I did. Something metallic clunked on the ground and I saw what could only be an expression of relief pass over the comic book villain features of Ike's face. Dandy looked even more relieved.

In a slightly calmer tone, Ike said, "Now get around the front of the car where I can see you. Come on, move!"

I felt like a kid sitting behind a big fat guy at the movies. I could only see half of what was going on. I assumed Framm did what he was told because Ike watched intently for a moment, then shifted his left hand from Dandy's waist to her shoulder and pushed her in front of him, moving to my right.

"The lady and I are going for a ride in your car. You make one funny move and she gets the first bullet."

With Ike's hand still gripping Dandy's shoulder, they moved awkwardly past my weed patch. Through half-closed eyes, I saw Dandy turn her head in my direction. She looked sad. Ike never took his eyes off Framm.

After what was only a few more seconds, but seemed like an eternity, they were out of sight, beyond the boulder. I rolled onto my left side to get at the Colt, and the world went wacky again. I grabbed the revolver in my pocket and got to my knees, each movement dimming my vision and threatening to turn off the lights once and for all.

From my knees, I leaned against the boulder and looked over the top of it. The scene was blurry, but I could see my Ford, no more than ten yards away. Framm was in front of the grille, facing the open driver's door. Dandy and Ike were on the other side of the door. She was in front of him and he was about to push her into the car. When he did, I would have my one and only opportunity.

Willing my eyes to focus, I watched Ike lean forward a little and push Dandy onto the front seat. The window in the door was rolled down and Ike's head was framed in the opening. I swung my right arm up on top of the boulder and aimed the Colt through a hundred layers of cobweb.

Ike must have seen the movement of my arm. He spun toward me and fired through the open window. I clearly heard the "pfut" sound a slug makes when it passes very close as I squeezed the Colt's trigger. I squeezed the trigger again and kept squeezing it until the banging stopped and all I could hear was the hammer clicking down on spent shells.

I didn't know who or what I'd hit, or even if I'd hit anything at all. My knees gave out and I felt the rough surface of the boulder sliding past my cheek. Then the lights finally went out, and they stayed out for a long time.

Twenty Two

9:00 a.m.—Thursday—June 10, 1937

The partially completed jigsaw puzzle floated in front of me like a flag waving gently in the breeze. The pieces that weren't in place yet were bobbing up and down all around me like they never heard of gravity.

I had a nifty miniature butterfly net with which to capture the loose pieces. Each time I successfully snared one, it would obediently jump out of my little net and into its place in the puzzle. I was enjoying the game and doing quite well at it. That's why I was a little annoyed when, with only two or three pieces left to catch, reality interrupted the fun.

I glared at reality, which took the form of a large red-headed woman in a nurse's uniform. She didn't seem the slightest bit sorry about lousing up my game, and to add insult to injury, she poked me with a needle.

I yelled, "Hey!"

Nurse Redhead looked up from the hypodermic she'd jabbed in my arm, gave me a smile that might have been friendly, and proceeded to inject some yellowish liquid into me. With that done, she dabbed at the hole she'd left in my arm with something cool on a cotton swab and left.

As my eyes followed her toward the door, I saw Dandy sitting in a chair. As soon as Nurse Redhead was out of the way, Dandy got up, leaned over my bed, and kissed me on the lips.

Since being kissed by Dandy was more fun than playing the floating puzzle game, I decided to stay awake and said, "Hi."

Dandy, in a fresh pink blouse and gray slacks, touched my cheek gently and said, "Good morning, Park. How are you feeling?"

I took a quick inventory and answered her question in a voice that sounded to me as if it was coming from a mouth full of cotton. "My back hurts, my face hurts, and most of all, my head hurts. Other than that, I'm groggy and I love you."

She grinned and said, "I love you, too, Darling."

I was kind of hoping for another kiss, but Dandy pulled her chair closer to the bed and took my hand instead. The bruise on her cheek was even more colorful than I remembered. I also noticed that her eyes were a little puffy, as if she hadn't had any sleep for a while. That made me wonder how long I'd been asleep.

Speaking very distinctly so as to sound a little less cotton-mouthed, I said, "What year is it?"

Dandy smiled again and I decided I really liked that smile. "It's still nineteen-thirty-seven, Darling. Thursday, June tenth, nineteen-thirty-seven, to be specific."

I mulled that information over for a moment and asked, "What time is it?"

She glanced at the tiny gold watch on her wrist. "It's a few minutes after nine."

"In the morning?"

"Yes, Darling, in the morning."

My eyelids drooped for a second before the significance of the time sunk in. When it did, I tried to sit up. Suddenly the throbbing in my skull went to full volume and the room dimmed.

Dandy said, "Park, what on earth are you doing?"

I carefully lowered my head back down to the pillow and said, "I've got to get to work. Kastner will think . . . ."

"Park, Honey, you aren't going anywhere for a day or two. Charlie is taking care of everything at the station, and I talked to Bill Kastner myself. I explained everything to him and he told me to tell you to take all the time you need."

That was a lot of information to absorb in one dose, and I must have drifted off while trying to sort it all out. I was disappointed when I woke up again because Dandy had been replaced by a young guy in a white coat. He sounded very friendly.

"Mister Atkins? Mister Atkins, can you hear me?"

I opened my eyes just far enough to see him and mumbled, "Uh-huh. I hear you."

"Good. I'm Doctor Phelan. How are you feeling?"

I glanced at the chair where Dandy had been sitting. I must have looked disappointed because Phelan said, "I sent Miss Harrison home for some sleep. She'd been here since you arrived yesterday evening and she really needed some rest. She said to tell you she'd be back this afternoon."

"Oh. What time is it?"

"It's a little before noon. I just came in to chat with you for a minute before your lunch gets here. Think you might feel like eating a little lunch?"

I thought about that and realized I was hungry, so I said, "Yeah."

"That's a good sign. In fact, given your condition I'm quite pleased with the progress you've made so far."

My mind was beginning to clear a little again. Since my condition seemed to be a subject of mutual interest, I said, "I'm glad you're pleased. Just exactly what is my condition?"

Doctor Phelan responded to my attempt at humor with a smile straight out of a med school class on bedside manner. He flipped a couple of pages in my chart and said, "Well, the most serious problem is your head trauma. We are fortunate in that there is no actual fracture of the skull, but x-rays indicate contrecoup intracranial lesions which are causing pressure on your frontal and temporal lobes, resulting in some neural disruption."

The young doctor looked quite pleased with himself for correctly pronouncing all those big medical words. I said, "Wonderful. Now, tell me what the hell all that means in a language I speak."

Doctor Phelan smiled a real smile this time. "Okay. When you were whacked on the head, your brain got sort of bruised from bouncing around inside your skull. The bruises are swelling a little and pressing against some blood vessels. That restricts the flow of blood to parts of your brain and causes some blurry vision and dizziness. Is that any better?"

"Much better. So what do we do about all that neural disruption stuff?"

"We don't do much of anything except keep you quiet. The lesions—bruises—will heal and the swelling will go down on its own. The same goes for the burns on your back. They'll heal all by themselves. We just have to give them some time."

"How much time?"

"Oh, a couple of days. If everything goes well, we can probably let you out of here on Sunday or Monday."

My foggy brain responded to that with an obvious question I hadn't thought to ask until now. "Doctor, just exactly where is here?"

He looked a little surprised. "I'm sorry. I just assumed somebody had already told you that. You're at Saint Mary's Hospital." Phelan looked down at the chart in his hands and added, "Room three-twelve."

Lunch arrived a few minutes later and Doctor Phelan left me alone to enjoy a thin slice of bland meatloaf accompanied by a few bits of mushy boiled potato and some tough lima beans. While I was eating, a short blonde nurse showed up with some little pink pills that nearly conked me out before I finished lunch.

My next encounter with the real world occurred in the middle of the afternoon. Will Framm showed up. The deputy was wearing a freshly pressed uniform, but he looked as tired as Dandy had.

"Hi, Park. How are you feeling?"

"About as good as you look. You ought to get some sleep, Will."

He smiled wanly. "I'm planning on it just as soon as I get done keeping you out of jail."

"Me? Who the hell wants to put me in jail?"

Framm sank wearily into the chair by my bed and said, "For one, the Marin County Sheriff's Department was seriously considering it."

"On what charge?"

"Well, there were several possibilities, but a couple of homicides were at the top of their list."

That surprised me. "A couple? I know Doherty's man, Alec, didn't make it, but who else do they think I killed?"

"One Ike Kawalski."

It took me a moment to recognize the name and another moment for my last few memories of Strawberry Point to surface. "You mean I actually hit him?"

"Three times in the chest, all grouped within a six-inch spread. Your other two shots probably would have been in there too, but he was already on the ground so they ended up bouncing off your car. That was some pretty fair shooting . . . Detective Atkins."

Nobody'd called me that in quite a while, and my expression must have told Framm that I wasn't happy to hear it now.

"Sorry to bring up old memories, Park. But I had to know who I was dealing with, so I checked you out. Why do you think I offered to go up to Marin County with you?"

I grimaced and said, "I thought maybe you'd just become fond of my charming personality."

"Not very damned likely," he grinned. "You had an inside track with the Dohertys. And once I had you pegged as one of the good guys, I just tagged along and let you do all the work. Besides, the way things were going, I figured you'd need somebody with a little authority to keep you out of trouble."

"So, are you?"

"Keeping you out of trouble? I think so. The guys up in Marin want a statement from you, but they seemed to buy my version of what happened out there, especially since Kawalski had a record as long as your arm."

"I'd be interested to hear your version of what happened out there, too. It seems there are some gaps in my memory."

Framm nodded. "I'm not surprised. Well, at first, everything went according to your plan. I returned the boat and called Miss Blanchard at your radio station. She agreed to stake out the intersection in case Davis got by us.

"I waited for her there until three o'clock. It turned out she got stuck behind an accident on the new bridge approach. Anyway, time was getting short, so I figured I'd better go ahead and cut the telephone wire so I'd be in position when you got there. Of course, you never got there."

"Don't remind me. I tried to shortcut our plan, but I wasn't counting on Alec being there. That's how I got whacked on the head."

"Yeah," Framm said, "I got some of that from Miss Harrison's statement. But at the time I didn't know what had happened to you. When the Buick finally came down the hill, I figured our plan was shot to hell and I was on my own. Since I didn't know if Miss Blanchard ever showed up to watch the road, it seemed safer to tail Davis and wait for a better opportunity. So I abandoned the original roadblock plan and followed them up toward Tiburon Boulevard, hanging back as far as I dared.

"Well, to make a long story short, your Miss Blanchard was there, alright, but Davis spotted her—either that or he spotted me in his mirror—and tumbled to the fact that we were on to him. He did a quick u-turn in the intersection and ran me off the road heading back to the house at about ninety miles an hour. I went after him and Miss Blanchard joined the parade behind me."

I said, "That explains the third car. When I saw you chasing Davis back to the house, I couldn't figure who was in the other car."

"Anyway," Framm continued, "I knew I couldn't catch Davis in that Ford of yours, and I was expecting a standoff at the house when you showed up in the middle of the road. I didn't think you had a chance in hell of stopping him, but you did and you know the rest."

"Not all of it. What happened to Davis and his wife? One minute they were in the Buick and the next, they were gone."

"Oh, you didn't see that part?"

"No, I was lyin' in the weeds, half conscious."

"Hell, I figured the Buick had hit you and you were dead."

"Not quite."

"Well, Davis and his wife took advantage of the fact that I was busy with Kawalski and took off across country on foot. Believe it or not, Miss Blanchard went after them in her Chevy! She'd have caught 'em, too, if she hadn't gotten stuck in a marsh."

I couldn't help smiling at the picture of Charlie bouncing off across the hinterlands in hot pursuit of Davis. I said, "That's Charlie. Have they tracked the Davises down yet?"

Framm shook his head. "Not as of the last time I talked to anybody, about an hour ago. There's an all points out on Davis and his wife, but they could be clear out of the state by now. Marin County has already notified the FBI"

My eyelids were starting to droop again. That annoyed me because I still had questions—a lot of questions. I pushed the grogginess away and asked, "What happened to Gladys Doherty? I don't remember seeing her anywhere out there."

"She was there. I found Gladys curled up like a ball on the floor in the back of the Buick. I couldn't get anything coherent out of her, though. She kept mumbling about how she'd killed Elaine. Can you make any sense out of that?"

Grogginess was getting the upper hand again, but I was alert enough to know what Framm was really asking me. He'd finally put the pieces together and gotten the same answer I did, which was that Gladys Doherty must have been involved in the blackmail scheme. He wanted to know if that was something he and the Marin County Sheriff should look into.

I focused on him as well as I could through half-closed eyes and said, "It doesn't mean anything to me at the moment. Maybe we can talk about it another time."

Framm nodded and said, "Then I guess I'd better shove off and let you get some rest. Give me a call when they turn you loose, and we'll have that talk."

When I woke up again, Dandy was back and the world outside my window was getting dark. Somebody had opened the curtains, and I could see lights coming on in the houses that lined the Golden Gate Park Panhandle.

We talked some about how Davis and Ike had been waiting at Gladys' car and grabbed them when she and Gladys came out of Lucca's on Tuesday night, but the conversation kept bogging down. There was something on Dandy's mind and I knew darn well what it was.

During one of the longer silences, I said, "I had a long talk with your mother the other night."

Dandy sounded a little angry. "She told me. Mom had no business . . . ."

"Yes, she did. Your mom's a pretty smart gal. I needed a good swift kick, and she gave me one."

"Park . . . ."

"No, let me say this. I'm surprised you put up with me for as long as you have, but I'm going to do my best to grow up and stop feeling sorry for myself. I may need another boot in the seat of my pants from time to time, but things are going to change."

Dandy was watching me with a great deal of interest. The sly little smile was twitching at the corners of her mouth.

"Damn it, Dandy, I'm trying to say I love you, and if you still want me, I'd like to try and work out our problems."

The sly smile spread into a full-fledged grin. Dandy leaned over and kissed me then she took my hand and said, "You aren't the only one who needed a good swift kick. Mom made me see some things about myself that really upset me, mostly that I was expecting you to be somebody you aren't instead of fully appreciating who you are—the man I fell in love with. So, yes, I still want you, and if you can put up with me, I know we can work things out."

We were still sitting there looking at each other like a couple of lovesick teenagers when the door opened a little and Jacob Doherty peeked in. His face looked drawn and he was surprisingly humble.

"I hope I'm not interrupting anything."

I said, "Yeah, Jake, you're interrupting something, but you might as well come on in."

Doherty took off his hat as he came through the door and held it in a way that reminded me of that old saying about "hat in hand." He stood there looking awkward for a moment.

Dandy made things a little easier for him by standing up and saying, "Here, Mister Doherty, take my chair. I want to go down to the gift shop in the lobby before they close anyway."

She gave me another kiss and said she'd be back in a while. Doherty held the door open for her and I watched with appreciation as Dandy's lithe figure disappeared into the hall. Jake sat down, and I wished to hell I'd told him to go away.

Jake was fidgeting with his hat and looking genuinely nervous. He seemed to be waiting for me to say something. I let him wait.

Finally, he found a way to start the conversation on his own. "Atkins, I owe you something, and I came here to settle up. Would the ten thousand I offered you in my office even the score?"

I was damn tired of Doherty trying to buy me off. "Is that what you think your granddaughter's life is worth? Or is that how much you figure it will take me to keep from telling the world how she teamed up with Davis to take you for fifty grand?"

I saw anger heat up his cold gray eyes, and I was actually relieved to have the old Jake Doherty that I knew and hated back. He seemed about to tell me to go straight to hell. I was a little disappointed when he got himself back under control.

"Atkins, I guess I had that coming, and I can't blame you for being angry. I'm a little hot under the collar myself. Still, Gladys is the only grandchild I have left. I can't abandon her."

"I take it you know the whole story?"

"Yes. She's here in this hospital. I just finished talking to her. But I started figuring it out after your telephone call yesterday. The questions you asked about the pictures got me to thinking. When I added up all the things that didn't jibe, I had a pretty good idea that she was involved somehow. I came over this afternoon to get some straight answers."

I imagined Doherty cross-examining Gladys. She was already feeling guilty as hell and I was pretty sure he hadn't gone easy on her.

"Is she alright? I mean physically?"

Jake caught the implication in my question. "Yes," he sighed, "she'll be fine. But it's going to take Gladys a while to get over what she did."

It was going to take him a while to get over it, too. I was glad I wasn't in Gladys Doherty's shoes. Still, she was the apple of his eye and in time he would probably forgive her. At the moment, though, Jake was more concerned about me. "Look, I've talked to that deputy from San Mateo. He either doesn't know Gladys was involved with Davis or he doesn't care. Gladys tells me that you figured it out and confronted her with it. The Harrison girl was there, but she didn't mention that part in her statement to the police. So it's up to you."

I couldn't resist making him sweat a little. "What's up to me, Jake?"

Angrily he said, "Whether or not you talk about Gladys' complicity in the kidnapping on your radio broadcast, damn it!"

"Jake, Gladys is your problem. My problem is that every time I turn around you're waving ten thousand dollars at me and trying to buy my integrity with it. That makes me mad, almost mad enough to broadcast the story out of spite. But that would just be selling myself out in a different way.

"The truth is I don't have a single scrap of evidence that points to Gladys. I know for a fact that she was involved, but I can't prove it. That, and that alone, is the only reason I won't implicate Gladys."

The relief on Jake Doherty's face was immense and obvious. He pulled a thick envelope from his inside coat pocket, held it out, and started to say something about still wanting me to have the ten grand. I interrupted him.

"How do I get through to you? Put the damned money back in your pocket. I don't want it. If you think you owe me something, just file the debt away for future reference. Maybe I'll need a favor someday. In the meantime, just say 'thank you' for saving your granddaughter's life."

That galled him more than anything else I could have said. The words "thank you" weren't in Jake Doherty's vocabulary and the idea of owing me a debt of gratitude grated against his nature.

Doherty stood up, stuffed the envelope back in his pocket, and glared at me. After several seconds, he managed to get the words out.

"Thank you, Atkins."

Watching the door close behind him, I kicked myself for not asking some questions, like how had Gladys managed to get Alec's help. Or, for that matter, how had Davis talked her into the blackmail scheme to begin with?

In the long run, the answers to those questions didn't really matter except to my curiosity. But I knew myself well enough to realize that I couldn't put any of it out of my mind until I had the whole story.

For the moment, though, the thing I wanted most was to see Dandy come through the door. She must have been nearby waiting for Doherty to leave, because two minutes later I got my wish.

Epilogue

10:00 a.m.—Sunday—June 13, 1937

By Sunday morning I felt ready to rejoin the real world I'd been watching outside my window at Saint Mary's for the past three days. The blurry vision and dizziness were gone, and my headaches were reduced to a level that was only bothersome when I made the mistake of moving too quickly. It would take while for the gunshot burns on my back to heal, but the pain was under control.

Taking these improvements into consideration, Doctor Phelan was as good as his word and tossed me out of Saint Mary's right after breakfast on Sunday. Dandy drove over in my Ford to pick me up.

Out in the parking lot, I couldn't help noticing that the Ford was quite a bit cleaner than the last time I'd seen it. I asked Dandy how it had gotten that way.

"Oh, your car's been parked at our place, and when Charlie and I got back from shopping yesterday afternoon, we decided to wash it."

"You and Charlie Blanchard went shopping?"

"Yes."

"Then the two of you washed my car?"

"Sure. Is there something wrong with that?"

"Well, no. It just surprises me a little, that's all."

"What surprises you? That Charlie and I are friends or that we washed your car?"

"Actually, both. I didn't think you and Charlie . . . that you two had much in common."

"Why on earth not? Charlene is a wonderful person and we have a lot in common since we're both in the news business and all. We've gotten to be very good friends."

I noticed Dandy's sly smile and said, "I think that's wonderful, just as long as you guys don't start ganging up on me."

With all the accumulated dirt and grime gone from my Ford, the groove Ike's shot at Framm left when it ricocheted off the driver's door was easy to find. The two nicks left by my missed shots at Ike weren't as obvious.

After watching me hunt for a minute, Dandy figured out what I was looking for and said, "They're in the door jamb, over here."

She pointed at two shiny spots of bare metal in the jamb where the door hid them when it was closed. I ran my finger over the indentations, and Dandy took my hand.

In a soft voice she said, "I was terrified, you know. I thought you were dead. Then I saw you stand up behind that rock and your expression scared me even more. Your face was all twisted and fierce . . . ."

"I was scared, too, Dandy. I'm sorry you had to . . . ."

She put a finger to my lips and said, "No, don't apologize. You saved my life. I got caught up in this thing all on my own and if it hadn't been for you, I'd be . . . ."

I kissed her hard, and the emotions we'd kept bottled up for the past few days erupted like warm champagne. She held onto me as if there were no tomorrow and I was just grateful there would be a tomorrow—hopefully, many of them.

We stood there holding each other long after the kiss ended. It wasn't until someone drove by looking for a parking place that we became aware of our surroundings again. Dandy found a hanky and dabbed at her tears, while I looked away, hoping she wouldn't notice mine.

She said, "Let's go home."

We hadn't driven very far when it suddenly dawned on me that I hadn't been to my apartment since Tuesday night. More important, most of my clothes were at the Mission Auto Court, if they hadn't already been sold to pay my room tab.

"I'm sorry, Honey, but we have to make a detour. My clothes are still at the auto court where I was staying."

"No, they aren't. When mom told me about that, I asked Will Framm to go by there with me and pick up your clothes. The clerk was very understanding when Will explained things. Your clothes are back in your closet now."

"Thanks, Honey. I appreciate that. I'll have to find a way to thank Will."

"He was happy to help. I got the impression he thinks very highly of you."

"Oh?"

"Yes. Will said he wished he had your instinct for detective work. Or something like that. I don't remember exactly."

"Coming from Framm, that's quite a compliment. He's a darn good cop. But don't tell him I said so."

Dandy chuckled. "That's funny. Will said the same thing. I mean, for me not to say he'd paid you a compliment. Men! I'll never understand them."

"Well, you gals do some pretty strange things, too. Look at Gladys Doherty. She had all the money she could use, and yet she tried to extort fifty grand out of her own family! What kind of sense is there in that?"

"It makes perfect sense, Park. At least, it makes sense when you know the whole story."

"What story? You mean to say you know why Gladys got involved in that scheme with Davis?"

"Sure. I stopped by her room Friday morning before I saw you. She really needed a friendly ear. Mister Doherty—Jacob, figured out that Glady was involved, and he gave her a pretty rough time about it Thursday night."

"Good grief! I've been puzzling over this thing for a week, and you come up with the answer just like that." I snapped my fingers. "What did she tell you?"

"Well," Dandy said a little reluctantly, "I shouldn't repeat what she told me in confidence, but I think you've got a right to know what started the whole thing."

"I think so, too. Now, why did Gladys get mixed up in Davis' blackmail scheme?"

"For the simplest reason in the world. She was in love with him."

"But Davis is married."

"Glady didn't know that. He lied to her about that."

"Okay, so she was in love with him. Why the blackmail?"

"Davis told her the sanitarium was losing money and would have to be shut down. He said he wanted to marry Glady, but they'd have to wait a long time because of all the money he owed people. Davis even told her he would have to leave town and go someplace else where he could earn enough money to pay off his debts."

"And Gladys believed all that? Even though the guy's drivin' around in a brand new Lincoln?"

"She was in love, Park. Glady believed Davis just like I believe everything you tell me."

I didn't care much for the comparison and said so. "I'd never lie or try to cheat you."

"Of course you wouldn't. I didn't mean it that way. It's just that . . . well . . . Glady trusted the wrong person. She isn't as good a judge of character as I am."

I glanced over at Dandy and she was smiling. I said, "Yeah, I know. And I'm a real character, right?"

"Oh, you know what I mean."

"Alright, so Glady loved this guy and he needed money. Why didn't she just go to Jake and ask for it? In spite of his tough act, Jake was a pushover when it came to his granddaughters. He probably would have given her the money."

"She was going to do that, but Davis talked her out of it. He said he couldn't accept charity from Glady's family."

"Yeah," I added, "especially since Jake probably would have checked Davis out before handing fifty grand and his granddaughter over to the guy."

"True. Anyway, Glady told Davis it was her money, too. Or, at least, it would be hers someday, and they would just have to figure out how to get some of it right away."

I shook my head in amazement. "Boy, that Davis must be one smooth talker to convince Gladys it was better to steal Jake's money than to accept his charity."

"I told you, she was in love."

"Yeah, so you said. Still, how did he talk her into something as goofy as a phony abortion? With those pictures and everything, it must have been humiliating as hell."

"I'm sure it was, but Davis made it sound like Glady's idea. She realizes now that he tricked her, but that's why Glady was so upset. She thought Elaine's death and everything else that happened were her fault."

I didn't have much sympathy for Gladys Doherty. Dandy did, though, so I kept my opinions to myself and pulled into an empty parking spot across McAllister from the Alta Apartments. It was good to be back in the Fillmore. Climbing the stairs, however, was another matter. They just about did me in.

By the time we got inside, my head felt like John Philip Sousa's entire percussion section was up there. I flopped on the couch and asked Dandy to hunt down the aspirin bottle. After I'd forced a couple of the chalky white tablets down my throat, she cuddled up next to me and we waited for the pills to do their job.

Eventually they got to work, and my thoughts meandered back to Gladys Doherty. Now that I knew how Davis talked her into the blackmail scheme, there was only one piece of the puzzle that still didn't fit right.

"Dandy, can I ask you one more question about Gladys?"

"Okay, but just one. Then I'm going to walk over to that great delicatessen and bring back something tasty for lunch."

"It's a deal. My question is about Doherty's houseman, Alec. I don't understand how Gladys roped him into this thing. I would have bet he was completely loyal to Jake."

"You sure would have lost that bet! Alec hated Jacob Doherty."

"Hated him? When I saw Alec at Doherty's warehouse, he acted like he'd go to the ends of the earth for the old man."

"He probably would have, but not out of loyalty. While Glady and I were locked up at that house—before I knew about her involvement with Davis—I was wondering what Alec was doing there.

"Glady said her grandfather knew something about Alec that could get him put in prison for a long time and Jacob held that over Alec's head. Glady thought Davis must have offered Alec enough money to help with the blackmail so when it was over, Alec could get away from Mister Doherty."

"Except," I said, "it was Gladys, not Davis, who made the offer to Alec."

Dandy nodded. "I suppose so."

Alec was the last piece of the puzzle. When he popped into place, I saw the whole picture for the first time. It disgusted me. I killed two men, come very close to losing Dandy, and an innocent woman died trying to help her sister, all because a silly society girl was so starved for love that she let herself be talked into a preposterous scheme by a greedy con artist. And Davis, along with his wife, was still out there somewhere, probably feeling sorry for himself because he'd gotten such a raw deal. I mentally ripped the jigsaw puzzle apart and heaved its pieces into the Bay.

After lunch, Dandy and I spent a quiet afternoon talking about everything under the sun, except Gladys Doherty. For dinner we listened to Harry Owens and nibbled on cold cuts and German potato salad left over from lunch.

Then it was time to take Dandy home. We kissed goodnight on her front porch and I drove back to the Fillmore feeling a little lonely. But for the first time, I had reason to hope that our future goodnight kisses might be exchanged in more intimate surroundings.

8:00 a.m.—Monday—June 14, 1937

The studios and offices of KDG hadn't changed in my absence. There was no particular reason to think they would. It just seemed like a long time since I'd sat in my squeaky old chair. Except it didn't squeak anymore.

I rocked back and forth and swiveled all the way around, but I couldn't get a peep out of it. I was pondering this apparent miracle when I noticed the little white can of Three-In-One oil next to my typewriter. It was holding down a note that said, "Park: Fixed your damned chair. Hope you don't mind! Glad to have you back. If you're free, let's have lunch tomorrow." It was signed, "Bill Kastner."

I was still sitting there in my quiet chair wondering why Kastner felt obligated to elevate me into his inner circle of luncheon buddies when the office door opened. There was something slightly familiar about the attractive brunette who walked in. She was wearing a pale blue blouse made of something silky and a navy skirt that was just short enough to show off a pair of very nice legs.

I stood quickly and was about to ask the woman if I could help her when I noticed the sheaf of yellow wire service paper in her hand. I looked at her face again, and she said, "Good morning, Park. Welcome back."

"Charlie? Is that you?"

For just a second, her lips formed a slightly sly smile that reminded me of Dandy's. Then she said, "Of course it's me, silly. Who did you think it was?"

"I wasn't sure at first. You've made a few changes."

"Oh, you noticed, huh?"

"Yeah, I noticed. Just like every other guy in the building, I'd bet."

Charlie sat behind her desk and sort of sighed. "Yes, I'm afraid you're right. I'm not used to so much attention. Dandy kind of warned me about it, but . . . ."

"Dandy? She had a hand in this?"

"Well, she just offered a few suggestions and helped me pick out some new outfits that are a little more . . . ah . . . ."

"I think the word you're looking for is sexy."

"Park! I don't look sexy!"

"Okay, if you say so. But I doubt if the rest of San Francisco's male population will be that easy to convince. I'll bet you've already got a date every night this week."

Charlie was blushing. "Well, not every night."

I laughed and said, "Alright, you can keep the new look, but go easy. This dinky office is already too crowded. I don't need every guy at KDG finding excuses to come in here and drool over you all the time. Now, let's get to work."

It was a relatively quiet day for news. Charlie worked on stretching what little of it there was to fill our broadcast, while I returned phone calls and figured out what to do with all the stuff that had accumulated on my desk since Tuesday.

I met Dandy downstairs at noon for a quick sandwich at the Owl Drug Store lunch counter. After that she rushed off to interview somebody or other and I went back up to the office where my trusty typewriter was patiently waiting for me to write the last segment of our Special Crime Report series on the death of Elaine Doherty.

Of course, my report would be somewhat anti-climactic because the goings-on out at Strawberry Point had been well reported on Thursday by all the papers and news programs, including ours. Still, I felt the need to tie up some loose ends for our listeners.

It took me longer than I expected to bang out the five minutes' worth of words that signaled the end of a week's worth of murder and mayhem. It took so long because I wanted to say something more than just account for three deaths, an attempt at blackmail, and a kidnapping.

When I finally pulled the last sheet of script from my typewriter, it was already close to five. Charlie returned from checking the teletype and reported that there was nothing new on the UP wire.

As she dropped the evening's script on my desk, I told her to take off and have a good night. Charlie came over to my chair, leaned down, and gave me a big hug that was accompanied by a kiss on the cheek.

The hug and kiss surprised me because they were way out of character for Charlie. I said, "Hey! What's that all about?"

She looked down at me without smiling and said, "Park, that's for being the kind of guy you are. I'm really glad to have you back. I missed you."

A moment later Charlie was gone and I was contemplating the fact that she omitted her usual comment about not lousing up her script because she would be listening. I gathered Charlie had something more interesting to do than sit by her radio while I rambled on about the day's news. That, I thought, was a definite step in the right direction for Charlene Blanchard.

At precisely six o'clock, Dick Stewart announced to the world—or at least, to our corner of it—that it was time for Parker T. Atkins with the news. For most of the next twenty minutes I told the big RCA microphone about the Michigan steel strike, the San Francisco hotel strike, Amelia Earhart's progress through Africa, and how Adolph Hitler and Benito Mussolini agreed to rejoin the twenty-five nation international nonintervention committee, thus ending fears that the Spanish civil war would become a major European conflict.

During the second commercial break, Dick Stewart returned to the booth and spoke some stirring words about the integrity and reliability of Crocker First National Bank. When he was done, I spent a moment or two bringing the baseball fans in our audience up to date on the standings—the Yankees were in front of the American League, the Giants were leading the National League, and San Francisco had one game up on Sacramento in the Pacific Coast League.

Then, after informing our weather fans that the Bay Area would continue to be fair and mild on Tuesday after the morning fog burned off, I said, "Now we bring you the final chapter in KDG's Special Crime Report on the death of San Francisco socialite, Elaine Doherty.

"Many of you may be wondering about this reporter's absence from the microphone during the last three nights. You were told that I was away on special assignment. That assignment was the kidnapping of Elaine Doherty's younger sister, Gladys Doherty.

"As if it weren't enough that the family of shipping magnate Jacob Doherty suffered the loss of their eldest daughter, they were subjected to even further tragedy when Gladys Doherty was kidnapped with a friend outside a North Beach restaurant last Tuesday night.

"Your reporter had the privilege of accompanying San Mateo County Sheriff's Deputy Wilbur Framm as he unraveled this complex extortion scheme. As Deputy Framm's diligent detective work disclosed, the perpetrators of this most recent assault against the Doherty family are none other than the very same people responsible for the cold-blooded murder of Elaine Doherty.

"The plot began with the attempted blackmail of Gladys Doherty, allegedly orchestrated by one Donald Davis and his wife, Mary Trevor Davis, former operators of the Twin Oaks Sanitarium in Mill Valley. The extortion scheme turned sour when Elaine Doherty intervened on her sister's behalf, an effort which led to her murder out on the Coast Highway at the hands of a San Francisco man named Ike Kawalski. Kawalski, a convicted felon and a member of Davis' gang, drove the black Lincoln your reporter saw strike and kill Elaine Doherty.

"When it became apparent that his blackmail attempt had failed, Davis reportedly renewed his efforts to extort money from Jacob Doherty by kidnapping Doherty's only remaining grandchild. Miss Gladys Doherty and a friend were held captive at a hideout on Strawberry Point in Marin County while Davis contacted Jacob Doherty by telephone with a ransom demand of one hundred thousand dollars.

"Your reporter is pleased to announce that the first break in this case, which eventually led to the identification of Davis as the person responsible for these heinous crimes, was the direct result of a lead provided by a listener to this broadcast. It seems that after hearing I had witnessed Elaine Doherty's death, Davis attempted to dispose of the murder vehicle by trading it in on another car at the Howard Automobile Company, located at one-thousand-one Van Ness Avenue in this city.

"As it turns out, the general manager of the Howard Automobile Company, Osgood Bledsoe, is a regular listener to this broadcast. When he heard that the police were searching for a black Lincoln Zephyr with a dented left front fender, he recalled that such a vehicle had been left in trade for a new Buick sedan. Mister Bledsoe promptly called KDG with the information.

"Deputy Framm traced the Lincoln's registration to Donald Davis and eventually located Davis' hideout in Marin County. Framm closed in on the Davis gang last Wednesday afternoon and affected the rescue of Gladys Doherty and her friend minutes before Davis was to make the final ransom call to Jacob Doherty.

"During the rescue, two members of the Davis gang were killed. The gang members who died were Ike Kawalski and Alec Deegan, a former employee of Jacob Doherty. Davis and his wife eluded capture during the rescue at Strawberry Point. Donald and Mary Davis are currently the subjects of a nation-wide manhunt, and authorities expect their arrest in the near future.

"In conclusion, your reporter salutes listener Osgood Bledsoe for his valuable assistance in this case and San Mateo County

Sheriff's Deputy Wilbur Framm for the perseverance he demonstrated in identifying Elaine Doherty's killer and safely reuniting Gladys Doherty with her family."

I paused for a moment, thinking a silent goodbye to the young woman I'd met just a little too late out on the Pacific Coast Highway. Then I said, "And that's your news for Monday, June fourteenth. This is Parker T. Atkins. Goodnight, San Francisco."

THE END

Meet H. P. Oliver

H. P. Oliver began his career with a degree in journalism from San Jose State University and spent the next twenty-some years writing award-winning entertainment and educational media. Now he applies his creativity and imagination to writing historical mysteries.

About mystery writing, Oliver says, "To be truly engrossing, a mystery needs a little meat on its bones—something more than just figuring out who done the evil deed. Taking a story back in time or even basing it on actual historical events is a great way to endow a good yarn with even more color and depth. Historical periods and locations give the writer an opportunity to take most readers where they've never been before."

H. P. Oliver lives in northern California and spends much of his time working on projects throughout the western states. In addition to his love of history, Oliver's interests range from vintage film to restoring classic cars.

For more about H. P. Oliver and his mysteries in history, visit his website at www.HPOliver.com.

More Books by H. P. Oliver

SILENTS!
Available Editions: Paper and Kindle

The Truth Be Told
Available Edition: Kindle

And The Angels Sing
Available Edition: Kindle

THE JOHNNY SPICER SERIES:

Johnny Spicer: The First Capers
Available Edition: Kindle

Pacifica
Available Editions: Paper and Kindle

Revolver
Available Editions: Paper and Kindle

For more about these Mysteries in History visit
H. P. Oliver's website at www.HPOliver.com.

www.ingramcontent.com/pod-product-compliance
Lightning Source LLC
Chambersburg PA
CBHW061137200626
46817CB00016B/1735